MusicFest was so much fun that we're planning another concert!

Mary-Kate and Ashley
Sweet 16

STARRING YOU AND ME

By Melissa Senate

≡HarperEntertainment
An Imprint of HarperCollinsPublishers

A PARACHUTE PRESS BOOK

A PARACHUTE PRESS BOOK

Parachute Publishing, L.L.C.
156 Fifth Avenue, Suite 302
New York, NY 10010

Published by
HarperEntertainment
An Imprint of HarperCollins*Publishers*
10 East 53rd Street, New York, NY 10022-5299

SWEET 16 books are created and produced by Parachute Press, L.L.C., in cooperation with Dualstar Publications, a division of Dualstar Entertainment Group, LLC., published by HarperEntertainment, an imprint of HarperCollins Publishers.

ISBN 0-06-052811-7

First printing: October 2002

Printed in the United States of America

Visit HarperEntertainment on the World Wide Web at
www.harpercollins.com

10 9 8 7 6 5 4 3 2 1

chapter one

"**Y**our turn, Mary-Kate—things that start with the letter *M*!" Jake said.

"Ummm, movies, mini-golf . . ." I paused, trying to come up with something else that started with *M*.

My boyfriend, Jake Impenna, and I had made up a game at the beach earlier in the afternoon. One of us would call out a letter. Then the other one had ten seconds to name all the things we could do together this fall starting with that letter.

Sure, it was silly, but Jake and I had just spent the whole summer apart. Now that school had started, we could finally spend time together. *Lots* of time together.

Like today—a perfect Sunday afternoon in southern California. We'd hung out at the beach all morning, sunning, swimming, and splashing each other. Now we were sitting in the food court at the mall, waiting for my sister, Ashley, and sharing a plate of spicy curly fries.

1

Ashley was shopping with our friends, Brittany and Lauren. *Shoe* shopping, which could take forever. But I didn't mind waiting—as long as I was with Jake.

"What about *munching* on curly fries?" Jake suggested. "That starts with *M*." He waved one of his fries in front of my nose.

I grabbed it and popped it into my mouth. "Mmmm. Thanks," I said, laughing.

"Hey! That was mine!" Jake said, pretending to be angry. Then he squeezed my hand and grinned.

I was crazy about him. He was gorgeous and athletic—star of both the baseball and basketball teams at Malibu High—and he was also sensitive and totally sweet. The two of us started going out right before school ended in June. But just when our relationship got off the ground, the summer came between us. We spent most of July and August apart.

Don't get me wrong, I'm not complaining. My summer had been amazing—probably the best three months of my entire life!

Back in June, Ashley and I celebrated our birthday with an awesome sweet sixteen party. For our present, our parents gave us a really cool pink Mustang convertible because—*yes!*—we had both gotten our drivers licenses!

Then my dad—a music exec at Zone Records— arranged for Ashley and me to work at MusicFest, a super-cool outdoor concert festival. We spent an entire month on our own, living in a dorm. We also made some really great friends.

And then, as if that weren't enough, Ashley and I both got parts in a new movie called *Getting There*!

It was *so* incredible—but I barely saw Jake at all. Now, as I looked into his amazing gray eyes, I was more than ready to make up for lost time.

"So how about a movie after school on Friday?" Jake suggested. He took a sip of his Coke.

"Sounds great—" I started to say. Then I paused. "Oh, wait a minute. Friday's no good for me. I've got a drama club meeting that afternoon."

"Oh, right. . . ." Jake dragged a curly fry through a puddle of ketchup and popped it in his mouth. "You're drama club VP this year. Cool!"

"It's better than cool. This year, I'm a junior, and that means I can try out for a lead role. Finally!"

"Excellent. We can go to a movie some other time." Jake snagged the last fry. "So what's going on at this meeting?"

"Mr. Owen, the adviser, is going to announce what musical we're going to do in November," I told him. "And I think I already know what it's going to be. Last year, he told me he was thinking of doing *Grease*. I'm *dying* to play Sandy."

Jake grinned at me. "The part is already in the bag. You're the best actress at school—everybody knows that."

"Well, *I* don't know it. . . ." I blushed at the compliment, but inside, I hoped it was true. "Anyway, if I do get the part, I'll be pretty busy this fall. Meetings, rehearsals, working on the sets and costumes . . ."

"When exactly do the movies and mini-golf come in?" Jake asked. "'Cause I'm going to be majorly busy, too. Coach wants me to switch to playing first base this year. Which means extra practices."

"Don't worry," I told him. "I'm not going to let anything get in the way of our time together. Drama club may be important, but you're way more important." I gave him a quick kiss.

We smiled at each other. It was going to be a perfect year.

"So, ready to take off?" Jake asked.

"We have to wait for Ashley," I said. I wondered what was taking her so long.

Brittany, Lauren, and I were sitting in our favorite shoe store at the mall, surrounded by tons of open boxes. As I was trying on my eighth pair of boots, I glanced out the window.

"That is the fifth girl from our school that I've seen holding hands with a guy," I said. "Does *everybody* have a boyfriend now?"

"What's the big deal, Ash?" Brittany said. "We don't need boyfriends. Especially when we've got

4

shoes like these!" She kicked out her foot to show off a thick-soled, pink suede sneaker with a silver stripe along the side.

"Oooh!" Lauren clapped her hands excitedly. "Those are excellent!"

"Absolutely," I agreed. "And they are totally your style."

Brittany's a pretty, African-American girl with cropped curly brown hair. She has long legs and a model-thin figure. Everything looks good on her.

I picked out a pair of black suede, knee-high boots and pulled them on. "I know we don't *need* boyfriends," I continued, "but I can't help feeling like the only girl in town whose summer romance didn't last."

"At least you *had* a summer romance," Brittany said. "I spent all summer baby-sitting. And there wasn't a cute boy in sight—at least, not one older than five! What about you, Lauren? Meet anyone while you were away?"

Lauren tucked her wavy brown hair behind her ears. "Me? Um . . . no, not really."

"And besides," Brittany continued, "that's why they're called *summer* romances. Once Labor Day rolls around, it's time to say good-bye."

I frowned, remembering how hard it had been to say good-bye to Brian.

Brian was a very cute, very special guy I met while working at MusicFest this July. He and his best friend, Penny, were awesome musicians—and really nice people.

Brian and I hit it off right away, and before I knew it, we were going out. He even wrote a song just for me, called "Blue Eyes."

I will never, ever forget the moment Brian first played me that song. It was a gorgeous moonlit summer night. Brian picked out a beautiful melody on his guitar and sang to me. He looked right at me when he got to the chorus:

> "Until I saw your eyes, I never knew,
> How pretty a pair of blue eyes could be.
> Until I saw your face, I never knew . . .
> That a girl could mean so much to me."

It was the most romantic night of my life.

At the end of MusicFest, Brian and Penny entered the festival's talent contest—*after* Mary-Kate and I helped Penny get over her killer case of stage fright. The night of the contest, everyone was nervous—but Brian and Penny actually won! And their prize was a real recording contract.

I was totally happy for them both. They had made their dream of a career in music come true!

But after the talent contest, MusicFest was over. It was time for Mary-Kate and me to head back to Malibu. And Brian and Penny took off for their own hometown, Seattle, to record their demo.

Brian and I tried to keep in touch at first, but our once-a-week long-distance chat sessions quickly dwindled to a few e-mails now and then, and that turned into nothing at all.

I was disappointed, but it was no surprise. Neither of us really wanted a long-distance relationship. When we said good-bye at the end of MusicFest, we knew that it was over between us. I had gone on a couple of other dates since then, but I hadn't met anyone quite as special as Brian.

"The good thing about a summer romance ending," Lauren pointed out, "is that it leaves you available for fall romances."

"And winter romances, and spring romances. . . ." Brittany waggled her eyebrows up and down and gave us sideways glance that made Lauren and me burst out laughing.

"You're right," I agreed. "And if I'm going to have an exciting fall romance, I should probably get myself some totally hot fall boots to go with it!"

I adjusted the pair I was trying on and stood. "Hmmm. I'm not so sure about these," I murmured. "They kind of pinch my feet."

"Take a little test walk around the store," Lauren suggested. "Maybe they'll stretch out."

I strolled to the front of the store and glanced in the full-length mirror there. The boots *looked* cool, but they weren't very comfortable. I wondered if they were on sale.

As I turned to head back, I glanced out at the people walking through the mall. I wasn't just imagining it. There *were* couples everywhere. Hand in hand, arm in—

Wait a minute. I stopped short. *That guy in front of the music store—why did he look so familiar?*

I blinked twice to make sure I wasn't seeing things. Because unless I seriously had Brian on the brain, I could swear that he was standing right in front of me.

But that was impossible. Wasn't it?

chapter two

I rushed up to my sister's table in the food court. "Mary-Kate! Mary-Kate! Mary-Kate!"

Mary-Kate glanced up, startled. "Ashley! What's wrong?"

"Nothing," I said, trying to catch my breath. "It's just—"

"Let me guess," Jake joked. "Killer sale at the shoe store?"

I shook my head. "It's way bigger than that. Mary-Kate, you will never guess who I just saw go into the CD shop!"

"Who?" Mary-Kate asked.

"Brian!" I told her.

Mary-Kate's brow wrinkled. "Brian? From MusicFest? Are you sure it was him?"

"No, I'm not sure," I said. "That's why I left Brittany and Lauren on the lookout while I came here to find you." I grabbed her hand and tugged.

"Come on—we have to see if it's really him!"

Mary-Kate glanced at Jake.

"It's okay. I really need to get home, anyway," Jake said. "My mom's waiting for me—I'm baby-sitting my little brother and sister tonight. Can you catch a ride with Ashley?"

"No problem," Mary-Kate said. She kissed Jake on the cheek. "I'll call you later."

Jake headed toward the exit, and Mary-Kate and I ran to the CD shop. Brittany and Lauren were waiting outside, exactly where I left them. They looked worried.

"The guy you think is Brian is still in there," Brittany told me. "But he's with a girl, and . . . um . . . they look really close."

"Look inside and see if it's him," I urged Mary-Kate. "Tell me I'm not seeing things."

Mary-Kate peered into the store and gave an excited gasp. "You're not seeing things," she reported. "It *is* Brian. And he's with Penny!"

"Excellent!" I cried. "Penny's just a friend," I explained to Brittany and Lauren.

I rushed into the store with Mary-Kate, Lauren, and Brittany right behind me. There they were! A tall, adorable, brown-haired guy, and a petite girl with long brown hair.

"Brian! Penny! Over here!" I waved.

They turned and saw us. Brian's jaw dropped.

He looked completely blown away. Penny jumped up and down. "I can't believe it!" she cried. "Oh my gosh! It's so good to see you guys!"

We exchanged hugs. Then Mary-Kate and I introduced Brittany and Lauren.

"I'm glad I spotted you," I said. "It is so incredible that you're here!"

"Yeah," Mary-Kate agreed. "What are you doing in Los Angeles, anyway?"

Penny's smile faded. Brian let out a deep breath.

"Uh-oh. What's wrong?" I asked.

"We're meeting with our record label in a few days," Brian explained. "Our CD isn't selling. Penny and I are making the rounds of some of the music stores to see if they have it." He pointed to the rack next to him. The CD, *Starring You and Me*, was shelved under the band name Brian and Penny came up with after they won their recording contract— Sweetbriar. There were four or five copies in the rack.

"The manager of this store told us he's sold only one of these in the past month," Penny reported.

I bit my lip. *I* had bought that one CD. It was sitting in my CD player at home.

"I don't get it," Mary-Kate said. "Your CD is awesome! Why isn't it selling?"

Brian tried to smile, but I could see that he was really upset.

"The record company isn't advertising it,"

Penny told us. "Because we're a new act. They said it's not worth risking a lot of time and money on an unknown band."

"But that doesn't make sense. How can they expect people to buy your CD if nobody knows about it?" I asked.

Brian shrugged. "I don't understand it, either. The worst part is, if our CD doesn't start selling soon, our record company might drop us."

"What?" I gasped. "That is so unfair!"

"Maybe there's something we can do about this," Mary-Kate suggested.

Penny looked discouraged. "Do you plan on buying about a hundred of these?" She held up one of the CDs.

"No, but maybe we can figure out a way to advertise the CD ourselves," I said, picking up on Mary-Kate's idea.

"I don't know," Penny said. "I feel funny asking you guys for help again. You did so much for us at MusicFest."

"We wouldn't do it to help *you*," Mary-Kate teased. "The world needs Sweetbriar's music!"

"I have an idea. Why don't you and Penny come over to our house tomorrow night?" I offered. "We'll think up ways to advertise your CD."

"You are just so amazing," Brian said. His gaze met mine. "I don't know how we can ever thank you."

I felt my cheeks flush. I knew Brian was talking to Mary-Kate, too. But for some reason, I felt as if he were speaking only to me.

"Um, excuse me." Lauren tapped Brian on the shoulder. "Would you two mind autographing these for us?"

She handed Brian and Penny two copies of *Starring You and Me*.

Brian and Penny beamed. Penny reached into her backpack and pulled out a pen. "Sure," she said. "Anything for the friends of our best fans!"

"Well, now we've sold *three* CDs in this store," Brian said. "See, Ashley? You're helping already!" Then he gave me a shy smile.

He's so cute! I thought. *And he still likes me. Maybe a summer romance could turn into a fall romance, after all. . . .*

❀

The next day at my drama club meeting, I glanced nervously around the auditorium.

"I don't like this, Mary-Kate," Nathan Sparks, the president of the drama club, whispered to me. "There aren't enough people!"

Nathan was a tall, skinny senior with thick black hair and black-rimmed glasses. He reminded me a little of Clark Kent—*before* he turns into Superman.

I nodded. "I can't believe it—there are only about eight people here. Where is everyone?"

Eight people! That was barely enough to build and paint sets, let alone fill all the roles in a play!

Mr. Owen, the drama club's adviser, glanced at his watch and stepped onto the stage. He straightened his bow tie and cleared his throat.

"Good morning, everyone," he said. "Well, I guess we'd better get started."

I glanced at Nathan. He sighed and shook his head. He looked as worried as I felt.

"I was afraid this might happen," Mr. Owen continued. "Many of our members last year were seniors. We lost them to graduation. And as you can see by looking around, membership is way down. Unless we can recruit more people, I don't see how we can stage a fall production this year."

My stomach dropped. Not put on a fall play? It didn't seem fair. I had waited so long for a big role. This was supposed to be the year I had a real chance.

The auditorium door opened, and a guy and girl walked inside. *Yes!* I thought. More people were coming. They were just late, that's all.

"Is this the astronomy club meeting?" the guy asked.

My heart sank. Two new members would have made a big difference.

Mr. Owen shook his head. "Uh, no. I believe the astronomy club is down the hall—first room on the left."

"Oh. Thanks," the girl said. She paused in the doorway. "What club is this?"

"Drama. If you're interested, feel free to stick around."

"No, thanks. I'm a terrible actor," the guy said.

I jumped up from my seat. "Drama club isn't only about acting," I told him.

"Yeah," Nathan added, standing up next to me. "We need people to design and build sets, to handle lighting, to work as crew—"

"Sounds cool," the guy responded, "but drama's not my thing."

"I'm interested," the girl said. "Not in an acting role, though. I love to draw and paint, so maybe I can help with sets."

"Great!" Nathan said. He pulled a notebook out of his backpack. "Leave us your name and number, and we'll let you know when our next meeting is. That way, you can still make the astronomy club meeting."

The girl smiled and ran over to Nathan to jot down her information. Once she and her friend left, Mr. Owen continued the meeting.

"Good job, you two," Mr. Owen praised Nathan and me. "If we *are* going to put on our fall musical, you're going to have to do more of that. We need a lot of new members. I was hoping to do *Grease*."

Yes! I nearly shouted. *Grease!* It was the play I

was hoping for. If I was lucky enough—and good enough—I was sure I'd get the lead role!

An excited murmur ran through the small group in the auditorium. It sounded as if other people loved *Grease*, too.

"But," Mr. Owen continued, "if we don't have enough members, we might have to put on a talent show instead of the play."

"A talent show!" I blurted out. "That's way too babyish."

"Sorry, Mary-Kate," Mr. Owen said. "We need at least ten more people. Or a talent show is all we'll be able to manage."

I glanced at Nathan. "There is no way we're putting on a lame talent show instead of an awesome musical," I whispered to him.

"I know," he said. "*Grease* is such a fun play." He flipped up his polo collar and slicked back his hair. "Don't you think I'd make a great Danny Zuko?"

I smiled. He was right. He'd be perfect opposite me—as Sandy! "So how can we get more people to join?"

"We'll advertise," Nathan said. Then he called out to Mr. Owen. "Mary-Kate and I are definitely going to bring in more members. Can you give us a week?"

Mr. Owen gave a thumbs-up. "You bet."

16

"It won't be easy, Mary-Kate," Nathan warned me. "And it's going to take a lot of time. We have to put up posters, talk to people, and really spread the word. Otherwise, you'd better dust off your tap shoes."

I fake-shivered. "No way. No talent show. We're putting on *Grease*. And I'll round up ten new members for the drama club if it's the last thing I do!"

chapter three

I tapped my pen against the spine of my trusty purple notebook. *Think, Ashley. Think!* I coached myself.

I drew a squiggly line beneath the heading I'd written: WAYS TO ADVERTISE BRIAN AND PENNY'S CD. Aside from the heading, the rest of the page was blank.

Mary-Kate, Penny, Brian, and I were lounging on the back deck of our house. We'd been brainstorming for about an hour. So far we had come up with a ton of ideas to get the word out about Brian and Penny's CD, but none of them seemed quite right. Either it would take too long, or we didn't have enough money to pull it off.

"I've got it!" Mary-Kate shouted. "What if we gave away a bunch of CDs in the food court at the mall? Then people would listen to the CD and tell their friends about it. You know—word-of-mouth."

"Good thought," Penny said. "Except who'd pay

for all the CDs we're giving away?"

"Oh . . . right," Mary-Kate said. "Forget that."

Brian frowned as he stirred the ice in his glass. Penny took a noisy slurp of lemonade through her straw.

I doodled a flower in the margin of my notebook. *Music*, I thought. Music, music—MusicFest!

"Hey, I've got something," I announced.

Three sets of eyes turned to me. "What?" Brian asked hopefully.

"Remember how many people came to Music-Fest to see the different bands perform?" I asked.

"Sure." Brian nodded. "There must have been thousands of people there."

"Exactly," I said. "So why don't you put on an outdoor concert of your own? It can be just like MusicFest, except you guys will be the only act!"

"But, Ashley," Penny said, "if no one's buying our CD, why would they pay to see our concert?"

I stopped. She had a good point there.

Mary Kate nibbled on her pen cap. "What if they didn't *have* to pay," she thought out loud. "What if the concert were free?"

"Hey! That's a great idea!" I exclaimed. I jotted it down in my notebook: FREE CONCERT STARRING SWEETBRIAR—BRIAN AND PENNY.

"I like the idea," Brian said. "But even if the concert is free, how will people know about it?"

"And where will the concert *be*?" Penny asked. "Won't it cost a lot of money to rent space in a theater or a park?"

"How about holding the concert at our school?" Mary-Kate suggested. "We have a huge baseball field with lots of bleachers. Plus, people can bring blankets and sit right on the grass, just like at MusicFest."

"That's a great idea!" I said. "And I bet our principal, Mr. Needham, will give us permission to use the field. He's big into school-spirit-building events, and he and I are pretty chummy. I did a ton of office work for him last year."

"Excellent!" Brian said.

"What about advertising?" Penny wanted to know. "How will we get word out that we're having the concert in the first place?"

"We can hand out flyers," Mary-Kate offered. "We'll hit the malls, the coffee bars, the park—any place kids like us would hang out."

"Okay," Penny said. "But will people want to come and see us if they've never heard of us?"

"Hey, Penny," Brian said. "They're trying to help. Quit being so negative."

Penny blushed. "Sorry, guys. I'm just a natural worrier."

"We remember," Mary-Kate said teasingly.

I drummed my pen against my notebook. "Hey, Mary-Kate, remember when Dad was working with that country band, the Dawson Brothers, a few years ago? They were brand-new then—nobody had ever heard of them."

"Oh, yeah," Mary-Kate said. "Dad got a country-music radio station to get a buzz going about them. The DJs talked them up—and even introduced them when they first played live."

"Wait a minute—the Dawson Brothers?" Brian interrupted. "They're huge!"

"Exactly," Mary-Kate said. "Once the DJs talked about the band, their CDs sold big time!"

"So why don't we get a DJ to advertise you two!" I suggested. I turned to Mary-Kate. "And who is the best DJ to advertise Brian and Penny?"

Mary-Kate grinned, picking up on my thought. "Definitely Wild Will Withers!"

"Who's Wild Will Withers?" Penny asked.

"Only the *hottest* morning DJ in the Los Angeles area," I explained. "If he talked about your concert on his show, *everyone* would come!"

"But why would a famous DJ do that for us?" Brian asked.

"Because if he listened to your CD, he'd totally love it," I said with a smile.

"We just need to get the CD to him somehow," Mary-Kate said.

"That doesn't sound easy," Penny remarked.

"Don't worry," I reassured her. "Mary-Kate and

I will find a way—no matter what it takes!"

"You guys are geniuses!" Brian cheered. "A free concert *and* a plan to get the attention of the hottest DJ in Los Angeles? If this doesn't boost our CD sales, nothing will!"

"Thanks," I said. "But don't forget, we have a lot of work to do if we're going to pull this off."

"Right," Brian agreed. "So while you guys are reserving the field and getting the CD to Wild Will, Penny and I will rehearse for the show. It'll be our best performance ever!"

"Great," Mary-Kate said.

"And I'll make up some flyers," Penny said. "Then we can all give them out."

"Excellent!" I cheered. I jotted the plan into my notebook. Then Mary-Kate stood up and gathered our empty glasses.

"Who wants more lemonade?" she asked.

"I do," Penny said. "Let me help you." She and Mary-Kate disappeared into the kitchen.

I smiled as I wrote the last line of our plan: GET WILD WILL TO LISTEN TO CD. It felt so good to be able to help our friends. They definitely deserved a big break.

"Ummm, Ashley?"

I glanced up from my notebook. "Yes, Brian?"

"It's so cool of you and Mary-Kate to do all this for us," Brian said. "I haven't seen you in so long—

I almost forgot how amazing you are."

His gaze didn't leave my face. It was the same look he'd given me in the CD store. I blushed.

Brian lowered his voice. "I really missed you, Ashley."

"I missed you, too," I admitted.

It was true. Now that he was here, I remembered how romantic and sweet he was, and how much I liked him. I could see us getting back together...but he still lived in Seattle. And I had already decided I didn't want a long-distance relationship.

Hadn't I?

I was so confused. All I knew was that my heart was pounding. I wanted him to kiss me.

For a moment, neither of us said anything.

Then Brian smiled and leaned toward me.

My breath caught in my throat.

"I'm back!" Penny called. She stepped through the sliding door, holding two glasses of lemonade.

She glanced down at us, and for a second, I thought I noticed a slight frown on her face. But it disappeared before I could be sure.

"Drink up," she said, handing a glass to Brian. "It's getting late and my mom's waiting up for us. We need to get back to the hotel."

Brian sighed and got to his feet. "You're right," he agreed. "We have a long day tomorrow." He chugged his lemonade and returned the glass to the kitchen.

At the front door, Brian and Penny thanked us both again. Then they waved good-bye as they sped off in Brian's car.

As I watched them go, a million questions floated through my mind. But mainly, I wondered one thing: Should Brian and I get back together? And if we did, how would it ever work out?

ACT OUT! TAKE THE LEAD! SET THE SCENE! I typed on my computer screen. JOIN THE DRAMA CLUB TODAY! NEXT MEETING: FRIDAY, 3 P.M., IN THE AUDITORIUM. SEE MARY-KATE OR NATHAN IN THE DRAMA CLUB OFFICE FOR DETAILS.

I picked an eye-catching font, then hit Print. A page shot out of my printer. I grabbed it and held it up in front of me.

Perfect! I told myself. *This flyer is sure to get lots of people's attention.*

"Mary-Kate, are you listening to me?" Ashley's voice cut through my thoughts.

I turned to look at her. She was lying on my bed, staring up at the ceiling.

"Ummm, of course I'm listening," I told her. It was only a little white lie. I heard her talking, I just didn't know what she had said.

"I asked you a question. Do you think Brian was going to kiss me or not?" she repeated.

"Oh, totally. It's so obvious he still likes you."

I hit Print again, and dozens of drama club flyers spewed out of my printer.

Ashley rolled over onto her stomach. "That's what I think, too. And I still really like him. But I'm not sure I should get involved with him now. It was so awful saying good-bye the last time."

"Well, look on the bright side. He's in town only for a few weeks," I pointed out.

"That's plenty of time for me to fall for him all over again!" Ashley groaned into a pillow.

"So? Would that be so terrible?" I asked. "You always say you haven't met anyone as special as Brian. Maybe you two could make the long-distance thing work."

"I'm not so sure." Ashley sighed and sat up. She grabbed a flyer from my desk and read it. "This looks great," she said.

"Thanks." I smiled. "Nathan and I worked out the wording at lunch. We're going to plaster them all over school tomorrow."

"Don't worry," Ashley said. "Between you and Nathan, you'll definitely get enough new members. And just to be on the safe side, give me a stack of flyers. I'll hand them out in all my classes tomorrow."

"Thanks, Ash!" I handed her a pile. "This just *has* to work. I already know all the songs in *Grease* by heart."

"And you'll be a perfect Sandy," Ashley added.

I grinned. I hadn't officially won the lead role yet. But no one else was really right for the part.

I'd been working in the drama club so hard for so long—Mr. Owen just *had* to give me the role.

The phone rang, and I snatched up the receiver. "Hello?"

"Hey, where were you at lunch today?" Jake asked. "I waited forty-five minutes for you."

Whoops! I winced. I couldn't believe I'd forgotten about my lunch plans with Jake!

"I am so sorry," I apologized. "I totally spaced. I was working with Nathan on the flyers for the drama club. You want to see one? I could e-mail the file to you."

"Sure, send it over," Jake said. "So what about tomorrow? Think you could have lunch with me then?"

"Definitely," I said. "I can't wait."

I just hoped Jake wouldn't mind spending part of lunch period pasting flyers all over school!

chapter four

The next morning, Mary-Kate shuffled into my bedroom. She yawned and rubbed her half-closed eyes. "Ready to begin Operation Wild Will," she reported. "Wake me when you need me."

I laughed as she flopped down onto my bed. Her hair was sticking up, and she had sleep creases all over her face.

"You have got to stop hitting that snooze bar," I told her. "You're twenty minutes late!"

Before we went to bed last night, Mary-Kate and I decided to get up one hour early to call Wild Will Withers as soon as he got on the air. Once we reached him, we'd tell him all about Sweetbriar, their new CD, and their free concert at our school. Then we'd make an appointment to drop the CD off at his office.

After that, everything would fall into place for Brian and Penny!

At exactly six A.M., I picked up my phone and

started dialing Wild Will's number. But at six-forty-two, I still hadn't gotten through.

"Here." I handed the cordless phone to Mary-Kate. "It's still busy. You try for a while."

I went downstairs to fix us some cereal. When I returned, Mary-Kate was totally awake—and totally frustrated.

"Busy, busy, busy!" she reported. "What good is an on-air line when no one can get through?"

"Let's just keep trying," I said. "Wild Will has to answer eventually."

I took the receiver and hit redial. "Mary-Kate! It's ringing!" I exclaimed.

"Yes!" Mary-Kate shouted, jumping up on the bed.

I heard a click. Somebody picked up! "Hello—" I started to say.

"Hello! You are the ninety-fifth caller!" a recorded voice answered.

"What?" I replied, totally confused.

"Sorry, but you are not our winner," the automated voice continued.

"Oh, no!" I cried.

"Please try again later," the voice said.

"What happened?" Mary-Kate asked.

"It was just a recording," I explained. I slumped over onto my desk.

"After all our dialing?" Mary-Kate asked. "That stinks!"

I lifted my head and nodded. "We're not going to get through to Wild Will on the phone. So what do we do now?"

Mary-Kate thought for a moment. "I guess we'll just have to come up with a new plan."

I glanced at the clock on my bedside table. "Not this morning, we won't. If we don't get ready for school, we're going to be late!"

❀

I sat in second-period English class later that morning and let out one of the biggest yawns of all time.

"Hey, Mary-Kate!" Brittany called. She settled in the seat next to mine. "What's wrong with you?"

I explained the whole morning to Brittany.

". . . so basically, I lost almost a whole hour of quality snooze time, and we didn't get through to Wild Will," I summed up.

"Bummer!" Brittany said. "What are you going to do now?"

I opened my mouth to answer, but at that second Ms. Tuttle, my English teacher, walked into the room.

"Good morning," Ms. Tuttle greeted the class. "Let's pick up where we left off in our reading of Shakespeare."

I perked right up. We were studying *Romeo and Juliet*—one of my favorite plays. Ms. Tuttle had us read the play in parts, which made class really fun.

I kept hoping Ms. Tuttle would pick me to read Juliet—and the day before last, she actually had!

I really got into the part. And some people clapped when I was done, which was totally cool.

"Danielle, why don't you read the part of Juliet today," Ms. Tuttle said. "And Devon, you read Romeo."

I reached for my backpack and rooted around for my copy of *Romeo and Juliet*. Where was it?

Ugh! I slapped my forehead with my hand. I was so rushed to get ready for school this morning that I must have left the book at home!

"Is everyone ready?" Ms. Tuttle asked from the front of the room.

"Can I share your copy?" I asked Brittany.

"Mary-Kate! Did you forget your book?" Brittany whispered. Her earrings jingled as she shook her head mockingly. "I can't believe it! That is *sooo* unlike you."

I made a face at her. "Quit teasing me. You know Ashley's the organized one."

Danielle Bloom, who was reading Juliet, took a deep breath. "I just need a moment, Ms. Tuttle," she said.

Every head whipped around to look at her. Including mine.

Danielle was staring down at her book. She had one hand up in the air, as if asking for quiet.

"Could she be any more of a drama queen?" Brittany whispered, rolling her eyes.

I smiled, but I had to admit I was impressed with Danielle's focus.

I had seen Danielle around school, but we'd never met. She transferred to Malibu from San Francisco last year. She was really pretty, with strawberry-blond hair and pale green eyes.

Most people just sat in their seats while they read, but Danielle stood up at her desk. Then she cleared her throat.

"I'm ready to begin now," she announced.

Brittany snorted. "Oh, give me a break."

"Go on, Danielle," Ms. Tuttle said.

Danielle took an extra moment before reciting the first line. "'O Romeo, Romeo! wherefore art thou Romeo?'"

I stared up at her. She was really in character, putting all her energy into being Juliet.

"'Deny thy father and refuse thy name!'" Danielle continued.

I couldn't take my eyes off her. She read with real emotion, real force. As she continued, everyone turned to watch her. She was so talented—a natural actress.

A natural actress, I thought. *So why she wasn't in the drama club?* Anyone who could read like that was usually first in line to audition.

Was it possible she didn't know about the drama club? If she didn't, she certainly would after today. Nathan and I had plastered flyers all over this floor between first and second periods!

Danielle paused to allow Romeo to answer. Devon wasn't exactly the actor Danielle was. He giggled through his short line.

Danielle, however, wasn't affected by Devon's performance. She read her next lines with emotion and intensity.

Wow. I was really impressed. She was a total professional. And if she handled a part in English class this way, how great would she be in a school musical?

As Danielle went on, still holding everyone's attention, I couldn't help thinking she would make an excellent Rizzo, the leader of the Pink Ladies in *Grease*.

Rizzo was the "bad girl" who thought Sandy was a total Goody-Two-Shoes. It was a great part, the second biggest next to Sandy.

Everyone broke out into applause when Danielle finished. I decided right then that I had to talk to her after class. With Nathan playing Danny, me as Sandy, and Danielle-the-Natural in the role of Rizzo, we could have an amazing lead cast for our musical!

Brrrrrrrring! The bell rang. I jumped up as fast as I could, but Danielle slipped out the door before I could catch her.

"Danielle! Wait up!" I glanced right and left. Which way had she gone? I caught a flash of her strawberry-blond hair and followed it to a section of lockers.

"Hey, Danielle," I called as I approached her.

She didn't turn around.

"Excuse me!" I said, more loudly this time.

Danielle turned to face me. "Yes?" she asked. She raised her perfectly shaped eyebrows.

"Hi, I'm Mary-Kate." I introduced myself, giving her my broadest smile. "I'm in your English class. You were *amazing* as Juliet just now."

"Thanks," she said with a slight smile. Then she turned away from me.

Hel-*lo*? I wasn't finished speaking yet.

"Uh, Danielle?" I said.

She turned back around and stared at me. "What?"

I pressed on. "I was wondering if you'd be interested in joining the drama club," I said. "We're putting on *Grease* and—"

"Sorry. I wouldn't be," Danielle interrupted.

"Wouldn't be what?" I asked, confused.

"Interested," she replied. "So you can save your little speech."

My jaw dropped open. This girl was possibly the rudest person I'd ever met in my life!

I took a deep breath. *You don't have to like her*, I told myself. *You just have to get her to join the drama club.*

"If you don't mind my asking," I continued, "why aren't you interested?"

"I do mind your asking," Danielle replied.

I blinked. Was she for real?

"Look, Danielle, you're really talented and—"

"I know," she said, flipping her strawberry-blond hair over her shoulder.

I stared at her. Was I actually having this conversation?

"Look, Mary-Sue," Danielle said.

I sucked in a breath. "That's Mary-*Kate*!" I said.

She rolled her eyes. "Look, Mary-Kate. I have been in summer stock for the past three years. And I have studied acting with *very famous coaches*." She spoke slowly, as though she were explaining herself to a three-year-old. "So, excuse me. But I am not interested in your little school play."

Then she slammed her locker shut and walked away.

I felt my cheeks turn red. What a snob! I never wanted to speak to her again!

But I had to sign up ten new members by the end of the week. And *she's a great actress.*

I sighed.

So I had no choice, I told myself. *I have to get Danielle to change her mind.*

chapter five

"So I practically begged Danielle to join," Mary-Kate told Mom, Dad, and me at dinner that night. "But she would barely talk to me! She came right out and said she was too good for a little school play."

"I don't understand. If she's so conceited, why do you want her so badly?" Mom asked.

"You should have seen the way she read in English class today," Mary-Kate explained. "She *was* Juliet. It was incredible."

"I think you're doing the right thing," Dad said. He patted Mary-Kate's shoulder. "And I'm proud of you for not letting your feelings cloud your judgment. Keep after Danielle. If anyone can get her to change her mind, you can."

"Thanks, Dad." Mary-Kate smiled.

I was glad Dad's pep talk had made her feel a little better.

Mom stood up and started clearing the table.

"Speaking of keeping after people," Dad said, rising to his feet, "I've got to make some phone calls. Although I'd rather do the dishes than talk to another radio station manager. Excuse me, everyone, this will take only a few minutes."

I glanced at Mary-Kate. Radio station manager! That reminded me of our problem with Wild Will. And it gave me an idea about how to solve it!

Mary-Kate washed the dishes and I dried. When we had everything put away, I grabbed Mary-Kate and dragged her upstairs for a meeting.

"What is it?" she asked.

"We need to figure out how we're going to talk to Wild Will about Brian and Penny," I stated.

"Okay," Mary-Kate said. "Do you have a plan?"

I nodded excitedly. "Dad does business with radio stations all the time, right?"

"Right," Mary-Kate agreed.

"So what do you bet he's got Wild Will's number?" I asked.

Mary-Kate's mouth dropped open. "Hey! You're right! All we have to do is get the number from Dad, and we're home free!" She moved toward the doorway. "Let's go!"

"Wait a minute," I said. "Dad's working right now, remember? Let's get some homework in first. Then we'll ask him."

• • •

A couple of hours later, we headed downstairs. Mom was in the family room, watching a video.

"Hey, Mom," I said, "Where's Dad?"

"He had to go out for a while," she said.

Mary-Kate and I looked at each other and shrugged. The two of us walked into Dad's office. We knew he wouldn't mind if we got Wild Will's number from his computer.

Dad's laptop was sitting on his desk—and it was open to his contacts. I scrolled through to the W's.

There it was! Wild Will Withers.

"Yes, yes, yes!" Mary-Kate cheered. She hopped up and down beside me. I jotted down the number in my purple notebook, and we raced back upstairs to Mary-Kate's room.

"Should we call now?" I asked. "It's kind of late for him to still be at work, isn't it?"

"Maybe not," Mary-Kate said. "And I'm too excited to wait. Let's give it a try."

I dialed the number. "KWOW!" a male voice answered. "Will Withers's office."

Yes! A real, live person had answered the phone! I covered the mouthpiece with my hand.

"I think it's his assistant," I whispered to Mary-Kate.

"So talk to him!" Mary-Kate whispered back.

"Ummm—hello!" I said into the phone. "I'd like to speak to Wild Will about an outdoor concert. I'm sure he'd be very interested in advertising it on his show."

"He's out of the office right now," said the voice on the other end of the line. "But I'm his assistant, Peter. I can take the message and have him return your call."

"Hi, Peter. My name is Ashley," I introduced myself. "Thank you for taking my message. It's very important that I speak to Wild Will."

"Are you a fan?" Peter asked. "Because I can give you the number for Wild Will's fan club. They'll send you an autographed photo and—"

"I enjoy the show," I interrupted him, trying to sound mature. "But this isn't about the fan club. I'm calling about a really great new band."

I gave Peter my cell phone number and Mary-Kate's, and Peter assured me that Wild Will would call back.

I hung up the phone, totally excited.

"He's going to call us back!" I announced.

"That's incredible!" Mary-Kate squealed. "Do you really think we'll hear from him?"

"Why not?" I said, heading for the door. "Peter said he'd call."

"Where are you going?" Mary-Kate asked.

"To my room," I answered. "I'm going to call Brian and tell him the good news."

I dialed Brian's hotel and asked for his room number. Brian picked up on the second ring.

When I told him that I had been in touch with Wild Will's assistant, he sounded so happy.

"Ashley, that is so cool," he said. "I just knew you'd come through for us."

"Well, I haven't come through for you yet," I reminded him. "I still haven't spoken to Wild Will himself."

"You will," Brian insisted. "You've never let us down."

"Thanks," I said.

"Listen—are you busy tonight?" Brian asked. "I'd love to see you."

"Well, I think Mary-Kate is tied up with homework, but I'll ask her if—"

"No," Brian interrupted. "I mean just the two of us. Just for an hour or so."

That familiar tingling feeling rushed over me. Something about the way Brian said those words made me feel warm and happy inside.

"Ummm—okay," I agreed.

"So, where should we meet?" he asked. "You know your way around here better than I do."

I suggested a cool coffee lounge that sat right on the water. "You can make your own s'mores at the table," I told Brian.

"Sounds excellent," he said. "Can you be ready in half an hour?"

"No problem," I said. I gave him the café's

address and directions, then hung up and flew to my closet.

I flipped through all my clothes and decided on my favorite jeans, a really cute ice blue tank top, and my pale blue mules.

A little mascara, a swipe of lip-gloss, a fluff of the hair, and I was ready to go. I stopped by Mary-Kate's room to tell her about my date. She was watching a video of *Grease*. She paused the VCR as I came in.

"You look fabulous," Mary-Kate said. "Don't stay out too late. I want all the details when you come home."

"We'll see," I said.

I told Mom where I was headed. Then I hopped in the Mustang and took off for the coffee lounge.

I got there right on time—eight o'clock exactly. I sat down at a round patio table with an amazing view of the beach.

Brian stepped onto the patio a few minutes later. He looked adorable in a crisp white shirt and khakis. His brown hair was still slightly streaked from a summer of sun.

Was it possible that Brian became cuter every time I saw him? It sure seemed that way.

I waved to get his attention. He waved back and walked over to the table.

"Wow, Ashley! You look really great," he said as he sat down across from me.

"Thanks, Brian." I beamed. "That is so sweet."

I turned toward the sound of the crashing waves just beyond the patio. *Maybe Mary-Kate is right,* I thought. *If Brian does still like me as much as I like him, maybe a long-distance relationship isn't such a bad thing.*

The waitress came to our table. We ordered iced mochas and decided to split an order of s'mores.

When our dessert arrived, we made a total mess toasting the marshmallows and sandwiching them between graham crackers and pieces of chocolate.

As we ate the gooey dessert, we talked and talked, catching up on what we'd been doing the past month. I told him all about the movie Mary-Kate and I had starred in, and he told me about recording his first CD with Penny. And suddenly, it was as though no time had passed between us at all. We were as comfortable around each other as we had always been.

"So Penny and I rehearsed like crazy all day," Brian reported. "We both really want to impress Wild Will. I think this show is going to rock."

"Wild Will's assistant promised that Wild Will would phone us as soon as possible," I told Brian. "I think he'll call us in the morning, right after his show. Then we'll ask him if he'll announce your concert on the air."

"Awesome!" Brian said. He took a sip of his

coffee drink. "You know, Ash, I asked you here because I just wanted to let you know how much I appreciate everything you're doing for us."

"It's no problem," I told him. "Besides, if I needed something, I know you'd do the same for me."

Brian leaned back in his chair. "If the record company doesn't drop our band, I might be spending a lot more time in Los Angeles, meeting with music execs, shooting videos—stuff like that."

"Really?" I asked. "That would be awesome! Maybe you'll even have to move down here—especially if our plan works and you guys become the next hot band!"

If Brian were in Los Angeles all the time, there would be nothing long-distance about our relationship at all. So there would be absolutely nothing stopping us from getting back together!

Brian shifted in his chair. "Yeah, maybe," he said. "So, did you notice that the song I wrote for you made it onto the CD?"

I nodded. "I was really touched when I heard it. I love that song."

"So do I," Brian said. "It means a lot to me."

My heart soared. Every bit of doubt that I had about falling for Brian vanished into the air. It looked as if this summer romance would go on and on. I couldn't wait to tell Brittany and Lauren—and Mary-Kate. I was so happy!

• • •

After a while, it started to get dark. We'd already had two iced mochas each, so we decided to get going.

When we reached my car, Brian gently turned me toward him. "Ashley," he said, "there's something I have to tell you."

"What is it?" I asked. I gulped in anticipation.

Brian stared into my eyes for a moment.

Say it, I silently willed him. *Say you want to get back together!*

But instead of saying anything, Brian suddenly shook his head. He mumbled something and stared down at his feet.

"Brian, what's wrong?" I asked.

"Sorry, Ashley. It's just—some other time."

I stood there a moment, feeling kind of stunned. What had happened? I didn't know what to say, so I got into my car and turned on the ignition.

"Wait!" Brian said, leaning down to look at me through the window.

I gazed up at him, wondering what he could possibly have to say.

"Ashley," he declared, "you are the coolest girl I have ever met."

"Thanks, Brian." I smiled, relieved. "So, are you free tomorrow night? We could go for a walk on the beach."

It was the most romantic thing I could think of to do. Like the night at MusicFest, when we took a walk under the stars and Brian sang "Blue Eyes" to me for the first time.

"I think Penny and I are rehearsing tomorrow night."

"Okay, what about the day after?" I asked. "We could go out to dinner, see a movie."

Brian hesitated. He looked uncomfortable. "I don't know, Ashley. Can I give you a call tomorrow?"

"Ummm . . . sure," I said. I put the car in gear, waved good-bye, and pulled out of the parking lot.

As I made my way home, I thought hard about the evening and Brian's strange behavior. *Maybe he was worried about the long-distance thing, too*, I reasoned. *I couldn't blame him.*

But all the signs he had given me—every single one—told me that if things kept going the way they were, I had nothing to worry about.

I was sure Brian and I would be dating again soon. And we would manage to make it work this time—especially if he moved to Los Angeles.

chapter six

The next day in the cafeteria, I stared hard at my cell phone.

Ring! I silently commanded it. *Ring, you stupid piece of metal!*

Mary-Kate sat down next to me with her tray. "I can't believe Wild Will still hasn't called!" she complained. "Are you sure he didn't leave a message on your cell phone during class?"

"No chance," I replied. "I checked my messages after every morning period."

"Don't worry, you guys," Lauren said. She and Brittany took two seats across from us. "It's been only one day. And I bet Wild Will is a really busy guy."

"Yeah," Brittany chimed in. "Maybe he's planning to call you back tonight or tomorrow."

"Or maybe we're getting the runaround," I admitted. "Maybe he gets phone calls like ours all the time."

"Let's not lose hope," Mary-Kate said, taking a sip from her bottle of water. "It's way too early for that."

Mary-Kate was right, I realized. I had to stay positive.

"Hey! Maybe you shouldn't wait for a callback," Brittany suggested. "I mean, what if Wild Will forgot your numbers—or his assistant misplaced them? Why don't you try phoning his office again? You know, just in case."

"Good idea," I agreed. "And besides, it certainly can't hurt anything!"

I pulled my cell phone out of my backpack and dialed Wild Will's number. Peter answered on the first ring.

"Hello, KWOW. Will Withers's office."

"Hello," I said. "This is Ashley. I left a message for Wild Will last night?"

"Ashley. . . Ashley," Peter repeated. I could hear him shuffling through some papers. "Oh, yes! Ashley! The fan club girl, right?"

I sighed. This was not a good sign. "No, this isn't about the fan club. I have some important business to discuss with Wild Will. Is he there, please?"

"I'm sorry, he's in a meeting," Peter said. "I'll have him call you as soon as he's free." He hung up before I could say another word.

"What happened?" Mary-Kate asked.

"Peter still thinks I'm calling about the fan club," I reported. "I have a *baaad* feeling about this."

Mary-Kate sighed. "Well, let's give him one more chance. If Wild Will doesn't call us back this time, we'll have to find another way to get Brian and Penny's CD into his hands."

"And *ears*," I said. "His *ears* are the important things!"

Mary-Kate laughed. "Hey, have you talked to Mr. Needham yet about the concert?" she asked.

I glanced down at my watch. "My appointment is in five minutes," I said. "I'd better get going. Wish me luck!"

"Good luck!" Mary-Kate called as I rushed out of the cafeteria.

A few minutes later, I entered Mr. Needham's office. His secretary, Mrs. Walsh, looked up from her desk and smiled at me. "Go right in, Ashley," she said. "He's expecting you."

"Thanks, Mrs. Walsh," I said.

Mr. Needham nodded at me from behind his desk. He was a tall, athletic man somewhere in his mid-forties. His thick brown hair was starting to turn gray.

"Good afternoon, Ashley. What can I do for you?" Mr. Needham asked.

I handed him a copy of Brian and Penny's CD. "Some friends of mine made this CD," I told him. "They have a band called Sweetbriar. And they're really talented. You can keep that and listen to it if you want."

"Thank you." Mr. Needham studied the black-and-white photo of Brian and Penny on the cover of the CD. "Is that it?" he asked.

"Not exactly," I admitted. "These friends of mine are also in town advertising their CD, and they offered to put on a free concert right here at Malibu High. If it's okay with you, I think it would be a really great show. Everyone in school could attend. And the baseball field would be the perfect place for Sweetbriar to perform."

Mr. Needham grinned. "That's a wonderful idea, Ashley! This kind of event can really build school spirit."

"That's what I thought," I said.

"Tell you what," he continued. "I'll give this CD a listen. As long as everything sounds okay, you've got permission to hold the concert on our baseball field."

"Oh my gosh! Mr. Needham, you are the best! Thank you so much!" I cheered.

I opened my purple notebook and placed a check next to the line that read GET BASEBALL FIELD FOR CONCERT! Our plan to advertise Brian and Penny's CD was definitely starting to come together.

And the success of our plan was now more important than ever. Because if we saved Brian and Penny's career, Brian could end up living in Los Angeles!

And if Brian lived in Los Angeles, then the two of us would definitely get back together!

All we needed was one phone call from Wild Will Withers....

"That's the last of them," I told Jake. He taped the final drama club flyer on the hallway wall. "Thanks for helping me."

Jake had eaten his lunch in five minutes flat so that he could help me plaster the walls with my remaining flyers.

"Hey, no problem," Jake said. He gave me a kiss.

"Hey, Impenna!" a loud voice called. "You ready for practice this afternoon?"

I turned. Vince Montana, Paul Quinones, and Andy Johnson—three guys from Jake's baseball team—were walking toward us.

Jake slapped each of them a high five. "Hey, guys! What's up?"

"Hi, Mary-Kate," Vince greeted me.

"Hi, Vince. Hey, guys," I answered with a smile.

"Mary-Kate, are you stopping by practice this afternoon?" Paul asked. "Cindy, Jennifer, and Lissa are coming, and we're going out for pizza later."

"Sorry," I told them. "I'm still trying to get new members for the drama club. I'm going door-to-door this afternoon until I've signed up enough people for every role, plus stage crew."

Jake frowned. "Really? I thought you said you'd be there this afternoon."

"That was before I talked to Nathan this morning," I explained. "Only two new people have signed up to attend our next meeting. I need to do some serious recruiting if I want to save this play."

"Yeah, OK. I just thought—"

"I'm sorry, Jake," I said. "I wish I could come. It sounds like fun."

After the guys left, Jake raked his fingers through his spiky brown hair and turned to me with a really disappointed look on his face. "Are you sure you can't get out of this drama thing?" he asked. "It would be nice if you could be at practice, see how I'm doing in my new position. Hang out, eat pizza— you know, normal girlfriend stuff."

I slipped my arm around Jake and gave him a kiss. "You know how important this is to me. Let's chat online tonight after your practice, okay? And I promise we'll do something fun together soon— once all this craziness is over."

"Yeah, sure," Jake said. Then he turned and walked down the hall without even saying good-bye.

I sighed. I'd make it up to him later. I had only one day left to round up as many drama club members as I could.

The moment the final bell rang, I raced out to the parking lot and jumped in my car. Ashley was hitching a ride home with Lauren so that I could get a head start on my door-to-door drama club pitch.

I knew exactly whom I wanted to visit first— Danielle Bloom. I also knew exactly what I was going to say to Ms. Snob to get her to join. I would tell her that the drama club desperately needed her talent. Without her, our production would be sunk.

The only problem was, I wasn't completely sure that my approach would work. Danielle had already made it clear that she knew she was talented. And that she didn't do "little school musicals."

At a red light, I glanced at the list of names and addresses on the passenger seat. I memorized Danielle's address, then continued on into the Hollywood Hills, past some of the most amazing mansions I'd ever seen.

I made a right turn onto Danielle's street. Aha! There it was, the huge house at the end of the street.

I parked, grabbed a few flyers from the backseat, and headed up a pretty, flower-dotted walk to the front door. I rang the bell and waited.

"Who is it?" The voice came through the intercom.

I leaned closer to the speaker. "Ummm, hi! My name is Mary-Kate," I said. "I go to school with Danielle. Is she there?"

A moment later the door swung open. A thin, dark-haired woman stood the doorway.

Whoa! I gasped when I recognized the woman's face. "I am so sorry to bother you. I-I must have the wrong house, or maybe I wrote down the wrong address."

Standing in front of me was Diana Donovan—one of Hollywood's biggest stars!

I started to back away.

"Wait!" the woman said. "You haven't made a mistake. I am Diana Donovan, and Danielle is my daughter."

I frowned. "But Danielle's last name is Bloom."

Diana smiled. "She uses her father's last name."

"Oh," I said stupidly.

"Danielle is at her piano lesson right now," Diana said. "But I'll be sure to tell her you dropped by. Did you want me to give her a message for you?"

"Um, yeah. I mean—yes, please." I stumbled over my words. "I'm the vice president of the drama club, and I've come to ask Danielle to try out for our fall production."

I handed Diana a flyer. "We're putting on *Grease*."

Diana smiled. "How wonderful!" she said. "*Grease* is a lot of fun. I did that musical during my own high school days. I played the part of Sandy. That's the lead, of course."

I nodded. "I know."

"Danielle loves *Grease*," Diana continued. "She has the DVD. She knows every song by heart."

"Awesome!" I said. I couldn't believe my luck. Diana Donovan liked the idea of Danielle being in our production. She was sure to convince Danielle to audition for a role!

"I wonder why Danielle hasn't signed up for the drama club already," Diana said. "I would have thought she'd be first in line."

"Well, the first meeting was only a few days ago," I explained. "I'm not sure Danielle even knew about it."

"Ah, I see." Diana nodded. "Danielle is quite busy with her activities. But I think it would be wonderful if she were in the play. It will bring back such memories for me!"

"The next meeting is tomorrow," I said. "The info is right there on the flyer."

"I'll make sure she gets this," Diana said. "You can count on seeing Danielle at tomorrow's meeting."

"That's fantastic!" I said. "She's so talented, and she'd be so great for the club."

Diana smiled. "Thanks for dropping by," she said. She stepped back inside the house and closed the door.

Wow! As I walked back to the car, a huge grin spread across my face. Diana Donovan was so nice, and she was going to see to it that Danielle auditioned for *Grease*!

I gave myself a little pat on the back for making a personal stop at Danielle's house.

Imagine! The daughter of one of Hollywood's leading actresses was going to be in our play! We were on our way to the most successful musical in the history of Malibu High!

chapter seven

The next afternoon, Mary-Kate and I pulled up in front of the entrance to Brian and Penny's hotel.

"I wish we could tell them that Wild Will called today," I groaned as I climbed out of the car.

"Well, we do have some good news," Mary-Kate pointed out. "Thanks to you, the concert is happening on the Malibu High baseball field! It's going to be amazing!"

"Amazing would be getting Wild Will to announce the concert," I muttered. "Amazing would be making Brian and Penny famous!"

"Don't worry," Mary-Kate reassured me. "We'll get to Wild Will somehow. And, hey, maybe Brian and Penny will have some ideas about how to do it!"

We pushed through the hotel doors and into the lobby. The four of us had agreed to meet at five o'clock that afternoon to discuss our concert plans.

I glanced down at my wristwatch. "Four-forty-eight. We're early. Let's get a soda while we wait."

Mary-Kate nodded. We headed outside to one of the little round tables by the pool.

As we weaved our way across the patio, we spotted Brian and Penny sitting with an extremely tan, good-looking man in a suit. No one at Brian and Penny's table looked very happy.

Mary-Kate must not have noticed. She marched straight over to the table to say hello.

Penny caught sight of us first. "Oh. Hi, guys," she said. "We were just meeting with Mr. McKenna. He's from the record company." She gestured toward the man in the suit.

Mary-Kate and I introduced ourselves to Mr. McKenna.

"Sorry to interrupt your meeting," I apologized. "We can come back later."

"No, no, girls. You might as well stay," Mr. McKenna told us. "We're about to wrap up here."

I slowly sank into a seat next to Brian. I stared at his face, searching for a clue about what Mr. McKenna had said before we arrived.

"Hi." Brian gave me a quick smile, but he looked worried.

"Hi!" I smiled brightly, hoping to make him feel a little better.

"Here is the information I told you about." Mr. McKenna slid a piece of paper out of his briefcase and handed it to Brian. "You can see for yourself that no one bought your CD in the last few weeks."

Brian stared at the page. His face turned white. Penny looked as though she were about to cry.

Mr. McKenna sighed. "I'm sorry, kids. I like your CD. I really do. And you're both very talented. But I don't think this relationship is working out for Sweetbriar or my record company."

He paused.

I sucked in a breath—because I knew what was coming next. Mr. McKenna was about to drop Brian and Penny from his record label!

"Mr. McKenna, wait!" I exclaimed. "Before you continue, I'm wondering—did Brian and Penny tell you about the huge concert they have coming up?"

Mr. McKenna squinted at me suspiciously. "No. They didn't."

"Great! Then *we'll* tell you," Mary-Kate jumped in. "Ashley and I have arranged for Sweetbriar to play a concert at our school!"

"Really?" Mr. McKenna asked.

"Yes." I nodded. "And it's totally exciting. We expect about three thousand students to attend the show!"

Mr. McKenna chuckled. "That's terrific, kids. But I don't think it will be enough to—"

"Wild Will Withers will be there!" Mary-Kate blurted out.

Mr. McKenna sat up in his chair. He stared hard at Mary-Kate, then me. "Wild Will Withers?" he asked. "KWOW's top DJ?"

I gulped and nodded slowly. But inside, I was freaking out! How could Mary-Kate promise that Wild Will would be at Brian and Penny's concert? We hadn't even spoken a word to him yet!

"We called Wild Will to tell him all about Sweetbriar," Mary-Kate babbled on, "and he agreed to announce the concert on his radio show."

"Plus Mary-Kate and Ashley can get Wild Will to introduce us at our performance," Penny added.

"They can?" Mr. McKenna asked.

"That's right," Brian chimed in. "And once Wild Will shows up at our concert, our CDs are guaranteed to fly off the shelves!"

Mr. McKenna sat back and put a finger to his lips. "How on earth did you manage this?"

Everyone stared at me, waiting for an explanation. "We—we happened to come across his private number," I said. "Once we had him on the phone, the rest was easy."

Mr. McKenna shook his head and laughed loudly. "Kids, if all this is true, I couldn't be happier." He rose from his seat. "Brian, Penny, let's meet after the concert. We'll take another look at where things stand, okay?" He snapped his briefcase shut and walked away.

When the patio door shut behind him, Brian let out a huge breath.

"You guys!" Penny shrieked with delight. "You guys are the best friends anyone could have!"

"And you have the greatest timing in the world!" Brian added. "Mr. McKenna was about to drop us from the label. Then you give us the news that Wild Will Withers is going to announce our show!" Brian gave me a hug. "You are amazing."

I glanced at Mary-Kate.

Amazing. Yeah, sure we were—*if* we could actually get Wild Will on the phone.

And *if* we could convince him to play Brian and Penny's CD.

And *if* we could get him to introduce Brian and Penny at the concert.

Those were a lot of *ifs*.

chapter eight

The next morning, Brittany, Lauren, and our other friends, Melanie and Tashema, sat around our usual table in the cafeteria, sipping juice and munching on warm rolls. Ashley and I had gathered the troops for an emergency breakfast meeting before first period.

"Okay, everybody—we've got a big problem," Ashley began. "Mary-Kate and I have to find a way to get Wild Will Withers to advertise Sweetbriar's concert on his radio show—*and* agree to come to our school and introduce Brian and Penny before the concert. The problem is, we don't know where to start!"

"He won't even return our calls," I added.

"If Wild Will won't call you back, why don't you try another DJ? Someone less famous?" Tashema suggested.

"Because someone promised a record company

bigwig that Wild Will would be at the concert." Ashley stared hard at me.

Brittany raised an eyebrow. "Yikes! You guys really got yourselves in deep this time."

"We know," I groaned.

"Well, instead of calling, why don't you just take the CD to Wild Will's office?" Melanie suggested.

"They won't let us speak to him on the phone," Ashley told her. "Do you really think they'd let us see him?"

"Probably not," Brittany agreed.

Everyone sat quietly at the table, stumped.

"Oh, hey!" Lauren exclaimed. "I almost forgot. There was a picture of Wild Will in one of my mom's magazines! I cut it out for you!"

Lauren pulled a clipping out of her bag and handed it to me. It was a grainy photo of a man sitting behind the wheel of a red sports car. He was wearing a baseball cap and sunglasses.

The blurb underneath the photo read, "When asked about his new toy, a red sports convertible, Wild Will Withers commented that he bought the car to match the hair of his longtime girlfriend, Anna Reeves."

I smiled and stuffed the paper into my backpack. "Thanks, Lauren. This is great. If we see anyone matching Wild Will's description, we'll be sure to flag him down."

"Don't worry, guys," Lauren said, placing a hand on my shoulder. "You'll think of something."

I nodded. Lauren was right. We'd come up with a plan sooner or later. I just hoped it didn't happen later—*too* late to help Brian and Penny!

That afternoon in the drama club office, Mr. Owen greeted me with a smile.

"Mary-Kate, you and Nathan deserve a big round of applause," he said. "Thanks to you, the fall musical will go on as scheduled!"

He handed me a list of names—and I gasped. "There are at least twenty people down here!"

"And they're all interested in joining the drama club!" Mr. Owen cheered. "Congratulations! We now have enough people to fill the roles in the play *and* volunteer for stage crew."

I smiled. "It was no big deal," I said. But deep down I was totally thrilled. All my hard work had really paid off.

I scanned the names on the list—there was just one little glitch. Danielle Bloom never signed up.

After talking to her mom, I was so sure Danielle would join. Maybe Ms. Snob had really meant what she said about "little high school musicals."

Whatever, I thought. I wasn't going to waste another second of my time on snooty Danielle.

Because now we had more than enough people to put on the best play ever!

"Mary-Kate?" Someone called my name.

I turned to find Jake standing in the doorway.

"Got a minute?" he asked me.

"Go ahead," Mr. Owen said, heading to the back of the room. "I need to make sure we have enough scripts for our next meeting."

Yes! I couldn't wait for that meeting! Once scripts were handed out, people could rehearse for their auditions. I knew exactly the scene I wanted to perform for my audition as Sandy, and—

"Mary-Kate? Hello?"

I blinked. Jake was staring at me. "Oh. I'm sorry," I apologized. "I was just thinking about something else."

"Yeah," he said in a low voice. "You've been doing that a lot lately."

"What do you mean by that?" I asked, stung by his tone.

"Listen, Paul is having a pool party over at his house tonight," Jake said. "He told me to invite you. Can you make it?"

Tonight . . . tonight . . . I searched my mental calendar and came up empty.

I wrapped my arms around my boyfriend and squeezed. "Absolutely," I said. "I can absolutely, positively be there!"

"Really?" Jake smiled, looking happier than he had in days.

"Really," I repeated.

"Um, excuse me."

I whirled around in time to see Danielle Bloom sweep into the drama club office. She squeezed past me—as if touching me might contaminate her with some ultra-disgusting germ.

"Mr. Owen," Danielle announced, "I'm Danielle Bloom. I'm interested in playing the role of Sandy— the female lead in *Grease*."

Sandy? I thought. *No way! Danielle was supposed to try out for Rizzo—the really cool* supporting *character. Not the lead!*

"Well, Miss Bloom," Mr. Owen said, "you'll have to audition for the role."

"Fine," Danielle said. She glanced at me and Jake. "How about right now?"

The next second, Danielle grabbed Jake by the front of his shirt and pulled him toward her. "Oh, Danny," she cried dramatically.

Then she leaned forward—and kissed Jake!

Smack on the lips! For an entire minute!

Mr. Owen's eyes widened. "Miss Bloom, that is quite enough!" he said.

Danielle didn't seem to hear him.

"*Miss Bloom!*" he shouted.

Danielle let go of Jake, who reeled backward.

He turned tomato-red as he fixed his shirt.

"Well, your reading was certainly . . . enthusiastic," Mr. Owen said, "but you'll need to come to this afternoon's meeting to pick up an audition script— and then to the formal auditions, just like everyone else."

"Of course, Mr. Owen," Danielle said in a sugary-sweet voice. She shot a look at me, then swept out of the room.

I stared after her, stunned. *What was Danielle's problem? What did she think she was doing?*

Mr Owen cleared his throat. "Well, I guess I'd better make one more copy of the audition script," he said. "I'll see you later, Mary-Kate."

I nodded and tried to smile as Mr. Owen left.

But I couldn't! I was too angry with Danielle.

No, wait, I was beyond angry. I was furious! What did she think she was doing, kissing my boyfriend?

Then a thought occurred to me—a terrible, horrible thought. Danielle was auditioning for the lead role—*my* role—the role I had dreamed of playing for months! What if she stole it right out from under me?

I clenched my teeth and made a decision. No way was that conceited role-stealer going to get my part!

"Mary-Kate? What was that all about?" Jake asked, his expression dazed.

Why had I begged her to audition? I wondered. *Why-oh-why had I gone to her house?*

65

I turned to face my boyfriend. "Jake, I don't think I can go to Paul's party after all."

"What?" Jake cried.

"I'm sorry, but you saw what I'm up against!" I said. "Danielle is looking to steal my part. I have to rehearse for my audition."

"Mary-Kate, come on!" Jake exclaimed. "Can't you bag it one night—for me?"

I took a deep breath. Why did he have to make this more difficult than it already was?

"Jake, getting the lead in *Grease* is really important to me," I explained. "Just like playing first base on the baseball team is important to you. I would never ask you to skip baseball practice. How can you ask me to skip this?"

Jake scowled and shook his head. "Whatever, Mary-Kate." He turned and stormed out of the office, leaving me all by myself.

"I've had lots of time to myself since the CD came out," Brian confessed.

"Really?" I asked.

We were walking on the beach together, holding our shoes by the laces.

Earlier, Brian called and invited me out to dinner. He said he was sorry for acting so weird the other night. He explained he was nervous about the concert. I told him that I completely understood.

We ate at a cute sushi place near the beach. Then we decided to take a moonlit stroll. We were so easy and comfortable with each other. I couldn't imagine a more perfect date.

"At first there were a whole bunch of appearances, and meetings, and photo shoots," Brian continued. "But then the CD came out, and everything sort of died down. That's when I realized how long it had been since we had spoken." He stopped walking and stared down at his feet. "I wanted to call you. But I felt kind of weird about it. I-I'm really sorry that we lost touch."

I nodded. "It's not totally your fault. Between filming *Getting There* with Mary-Kate, and going back to school, I didn't have any time to get in touch with you, either."

"Ashley, I've never stopped thinking about you," Brian admitted. "From the moment we said good-bye."

I couldn't speak, even if I knew what to say. I looked into his eyes, feeling just about ready to burst.

"Ashley—I would be so happy if we could be a couple again, but—"

He stopped—and stared out at the ocean. I waited, but he didn't seem to know how to go on.

"Brian, is it the long-distance thing?" I asked.

He shifted nervously from one foot to the other.

"It bothered me, too, at first," I continued. "I

didn't want to have to say good-bye to you all over again. But then you said that if your CD takes off, you'll be here a lot more often and . . ."

I took a deep breath. This was the really hard part. ". . . and I realized something, too. It doesn't matter to me if we're apart sometimes. I'd just like to be with you."

He turned to face me. I tried to read all the different emotions in his eyes.

Then he reached out and gently pushed a lock of my hair behind my ear. A tingle danced up my spine. He was quiet, just staring into my eyes.

And then he kissed me.

It was the most unforgettable kiss I'd ever experienced.

chapter nine

"**H**e is the most amazing kisser," Ashley said in a dreamy voice. "Did I mention that?"

"What?" I asked, trying to pay attention to the audition script on my lap.

I was sitting at my desk, deep in concentration, trying to perfect my audition. Now that Ashley was home from her date, she was ready to spill the details.

Normally, I'd be ready to dish. But tonight I was still fuming over Danielle.

That snobby redhead, I thought. *She caused the fight between Jake and me.*

She—

Wait a minute. That *redhead* . . .

I reached into my backpack and pulled out the clipping of Wild Will that Lauren had given me. I stared at the picture—and the caption underneath it.

"That's it!" I shouted.

"What's it?" Ashley asked.

I jumped on top of my bed. "Ashley! I can't believe this! I just figured out how to get Wild Will to listen to Brian and Penny's CD!"

Ashley sat up straighter. "How?" she asked.

I waggled my eyebrows. "Tomorrow afternoon, you and I are going to ambush him!"

"Mary-Kate, do we really have to crouch down behind this dusty old car?" I asked. "My shirt is getting dirty and—yeow!—my legs are starting to cramp!"

The two of us were staked out in KWOW's parking garage, waiting for a certain famous DJ to leave the office for the day.

Mary-Kate's plan to ambush Wild Will was brilliant. We had a picture of his brand-new red sports car from the magazine article that Lauren gave us. We found it and waited. The moment Wild Will approached his car, Mary-Kate and I would pounce!

We'd introduce ourselves, hand Wild Will Brian and Penny's CD, and tell him all about the concert. Once he listened to Sweetbriar's awesome sound, the rest would be history!

"Yes, we *do* have to hide here," Mary-Kate said. "Because this is the best place to keep an eye on Wild Will's car!" She pointed across the aisle to a cherry red convertible.

"But why can't we just stand up like normal people?" I asked.

"Because we don't want Wild Will to think we're stalking him," Mary-Kate explained.

"We *are* stalking him," I argued.

"Shhh!" Mary-Kate interrupted me. "Someone's coming!"

A man in his late thirties walked down the garage ramp toward us. He whistled to himself, tossing his car keys up in the air and catching them on the way down.

Excellent, I thought. If that is Wild Will, he is definitely in a good mood!

I peeked up over the hood of the car. The man had brown, curly hair and fair skin—just like Wild Will. But he was dressed kind of strangely—in a tan suit and a striped tie. It wasn't at all what I would have expected. But then, what did I know about how DJs dressed?

His footsteps echoed as he made his way down the aisle. Mary-Kate grabbed my hand excitedly. Was it Wild Will? Was he headed toward the red sports car?

The man pressed a button on his key chain.

Beep-beep! The lights on the red sports car blinked.

Yes! It was Wild Will!

"Let's go!" Mary-Kate shouted.

We sprung up from our hiding place and ran over to Wild Will. "Excuse me!" I called.

The man turned, startled.

"Sorry to bother you." I pressed a copy of Sweetbriar's CD in Wild Will's hand. "But you have *got* to listen to this CD. It's amazing! Sweetbriar is this really talented band."

Wild Will glanced down at the CD. "Sweetbriar? Never heard of them."

"We know," Mary-Kate chimed in. "But once you listen to their songs, you are going to love them!"

"You think?" Wild Will asked. He turned over the CD and read the names of the tracks. "All right. I'll give them a chance. I was in the mood to listen to something new today, anyway."

Mary-Kate and I beamed.

Wild Will opened the car door, sat down in the driver's seat, and popped the CD into the player. Then he rolled down his windows.

As the first track played, I felt ready to burst with happiness. *Wild Will is actually listening to Brian and Penny's CD!* I thought. *How cool is that?*

"Sounds great!" he said, nodding his head to the beat. "Really good."

"So you'll come to Sweetbriar's free concert?" I asked him.

"And you'll announce it on your morning show?" Mary-Kate added.

Wild Will looked totally confused.

"Morning show?" he asked.

I glanced at Mary-Kate. Suddenly, I had a sinking feeling in my stomach.

"Um, aren't you Wild Will, the DJ?" Mary-Kate asked.

The man laughed. "No. I'm Dave Sanders, an accountant for the radio station."

Our faces must have totally fallen.

"Sorry to disappoint you," he said.

"We were really hoping to talk to Wild Will," I explained. "Doesn't he park his red sports car in this lot?"

"Nah," the guy said. "I hear he gets driven to and from the station every day."

I slapped my forehead with my hand. Of course he had a driver. He was Wild Will!

"Well, anyway, thanks for the CD, girls!" the accountant added.

"You're welcome," I muttered.

He put the car in gear and pulled away.

"Hey, wait!" Mary-Kate yelled as the car squealed out of the garage. "Wait! That's *my* CD!"

chapter ten

"These posters Penny made are awesome!" I exclaimed. "If it wasn't free, this concert would be sold out!"

Mary-Kate and I spent an hour after school on Monday plastering huge posters about Brian and Penny's concert over every available surface.

People kept coming up to us to ask about Sweetbriar's concert. The baseball field was going to be packed!

"But still," Mary-Kate warned, "we have to get to Wild Will—right away. If he doesn't show up at the concert, Mr. McKenna will drop Brian and Penny for sure."

"Don't remind me." I groaned. "We need a new plan. But what?"

Mary-Kate glanced at her watch. "We'll have to figure that out later. Auditions start in five minutes. And that Danielle is going after the role of Sandy!"

I grabbed Mary-Kate by the shoulders and gave her a shake. "Hey. You're going to do great," I assured her. "And if Mr. Owen is casting the show, you have nothing to worry about. He's your biggest fan!"

"I *wish* it was Mr. Owen," Mary-Kate said. "But he's just one of a four-person panel—there are two other teachers *and* the assistant principal."

"You'll knock 'em dead, Mary-Kate," I coached her, and I knew she would. But I could tell she had something else on her mind.

"Have you talked to Jake today?" I asked her.

She shook her head. "We haven't spoken since last week."

"You'll work it out," I assured her.

"I hope so."

"Go on." I pushed her down the hallway. "Get out there and break a leg." She began to jog toward the auditorium. "Not really!" I called after her.

Poor Mary-Kate, I thought. She had so much going on right now. Between Danielle, auditions, and the concert, she could really use the support of her boyfriend about now.

And speaking of boyfriends . . .

I pulled out my cell phone and dialed Brian's hotel. It had been a couple of days since our date, but I couldn't get that perfect, totally amazing kiss out of my mind. I just had to talk to him.

I continued posting flyers as the phone rang in my ear. After five rings, I gave up. No answer. And I didn't want to leave another message on the hotel voice mail.

We hadn't spoken in a couple of days. Where could he be?

He's probably just busy, I told myself. *Don't let it worry you.*

Besides, I had much bigger worries. Like how I was going to make sure that Wild Will showed up at this concert!

I had to get him there—for Brian—no matter what!

I entered the auditorium and glanced around.

Danielle fixed me in her steely gaze, staring me down. Trying to intimidate me.

Great. As if fighting with Jake weren't bad enough, now I had to contend with Ms. My-Mom-Is-a-Superstar-Actress-and-I'm-Going-to-Be-One-Too.

Don't let her get to you, I told myself. *You're totally prepared for this audition. You've been rehearsing like crazy. You're ready!*

Feeling pumped, I checked out the competition aside from Danielle. Four other girls were auditioning for the role of Sandy.

The auditorium was packed. All the drama club

members were there, even those who weren't auditioning for roles. I took a seat next to Brittany, who was auditioning to be a Pink Lady.

I grabbed my script from my backpack and glanced at the first row. Three of the judges sat there, notebooks open and pens ready—an English teacher named Ms. Wesley; the music teacher, Mr. Harnauer; and the assistant principal, Ms. Greenberg.

Mr. Owen stepped onstage. "Welcome to the auditions for the fall musical, *Grease!*" he announced. Everyone clapped.

Mr. Owen held his notebook open in front of him. He read out all the parts and the number of people auditioning for those parts. He mentioned six hopeful Sandys, five Rizzos, and a lot of Pink Ladies.

"And for the part of Danny Zuko," Mr. Owen concluded, "two young men will be auditioning."

Wait a minute. *Two* young men?

The people around me started buzzing. As of yesterday, only Nathan had signed up to try out for Danny. He was a senior and a talented actor— everyone thought he was the only choice for the lead male role.

"I wonder who the other guy is," I whispered to Brittany.

"Could it be Kevin or Lee?" Brittany suggested, naming two boys who had signed up for smaller parts. "Maybe one of them got up the courage to face off against Nathan."

It would take a lot of courage, I thought. Nathan was that good.

"And now, let's have our first audition for the part of Sandy," Mr. Owen said. "Danielle Bloom."

I gripped the armrests of my seat. Danielle took her time getting up from her chair—of course. Then she waltzed dramatically to the stage.

"I'll be ready in moment, Mr. Owen," she called. She closed her eyes and raised an arm in the air as though she were an Olympic gymnast. Then she opened her eyes again. "I'll begin now."

Brittany rolled her eyes. "Do you believe her?"

As expected, Danielle was great. Her voice was strong, yet full of Sandy's hopeful emotion. In front of my eyes, I watched Danielle morph from a conceited snob to a 1950s Goody-Two-Shoes who was crazy about a boy. She was mesmerizing.

My stomach filled with butterflies. I was glad I'd chosen a different scene to perform.

As Danielle left the stage, the audience broke out into applause. It went on and on. I groaned and shifted in my seat. Why, oh why did I seek this girl out? I practically begged her to audition. What was I thinking?

You were thinking of the good of the drama club, I reminded myself. And besides, competition is good. Competition is healthy.

Competition will keep you up at night!

Mr. Owen called up two other Sandys—a sophomore and senior. They each got a smattering of polite applause—not as much as Danielle got. I was up next. The butterflies fluttered around in my stomach.

Mr. Owen took the stage and glanced at the sheet of paper in his hand. "Okay, how about we shake things up a bit? Let's have one of our Dannys audition next. Mr. Impenna, why don't you go first?"

Mr. Impenna?

I stared in total shock as Jake jogged up the few steps to the stage. What was this all about? Was Jake auditioning for the play? Why?

"You can begin anytime you're ready, Jake," Mr. Owen said.

A moment passed. I felt Brittany's eyes on me. "What is he doing?" she whispered. "Why isn't he saying anything?"

I shook my head. I had no idea.

"Um, I decided to try out at the last minute," Jake told the panel of judges. "So I haven't memorized a scene from the play or anything."

"That's all right," Mr. Owen said. "You may do anything you like, as long as it gives us a sense of your singing and acting abilities."

"Cool," Jake said. He thought for a moment.

"Oh, yeah, I've got something. This is a song I performed at a spring festival several years ago. It really brought the house down."

What spring festival? I wondered. *When did he ever sing at a festival?*

He stood in the middle of the stage and cleared his throat.

"I'm a little teapot, short and stout," Jake sang. He put his hands on his hips, miming the teapot. *"Here is my handle, here is my spout . . ."*

I slunk down in my chair, covering my face with my script. *Oh, no. He's* not *doing this to me. He's not singing "I'm a Little Teapot" in front of my entire drama club!*

I peeked over my script at the stage.

"When I get all steamed up, hear me shout . . ."

It's true, I thought. *This isn't a nightmare. It's really happening!*

". . . tip me over and pour me out!"

Jake finished the number. Everyone in the audience snickered. From the back, some of the boys clapped and whistled. The judges sat in stony silence.

Finally, Mr. Owen climbed onto the stage. "Thank you, Mr. Impenna. That was—unusual." Jake grinned and took a bow.

This is nothing but a big joke to him, I thought. *He thinks he's funny!*

Just what was he trying to prove?

I was furious. So furious that I could feel my cheeks burning red.

Jake stepped off the stage and came over to me. I threw my script on my chair and dragged him to the back of the auditorium.

"Jake! What was that all about?" I demanded.

Jake looked surprised at the anger in my voice. "Whoa. Calm down, Mary-Kate. I just auditioned for the play."

"That was an audition?" I shouted. "You sang a kiddie song!"

"I know," Jake said. "It's the only thing I've ever sung onstage before, so I figured it was safe. I was the star of my first grade play, you know."

"Let me guess," I snapped. "At the spring festival? *Twelve years ago?*"

"Right," Jake said. "Come on, Mary-Kate. You know I'm not a great actor. But I think I showed those judges that I'm willing to do just about anything to be in the play."

"You don't want to be in the play," I said. "You came here to make fun of me! How could you do that?"

Jake shook his head. "You don't understand, Mary-Kate."

"Then explain why—"

"Because I felt bad about our fight the other day," Jake interrupted. "Because we haven't been spending enough time together." His voice started getting louder and louder. "I thought if I joined the drama club, it would fix the problem. But you're too wrapped up in yourself to see any of that."

Jake paused, then said quietly, "See you around, Mary-Kate."

He turned quickly and walked away.

Before I could even decide if I should go after him, Mr. Owen called my name.

It was my turn to audition.

I pressed my hands against my forehead. *Get yourself together!* I told myself. *This is it! The moment you've been waiting for!*

Slowly, calmly, I walked back toward the front of the auditorium. I climbed up the steps to the stage.

I gazed out at the sea of faces. Everyone was watching me, waiting for me to start.

I took a long, deep breath—and began.

chapter eleven

"Cheer up, Mary-Kate!" I said. "You did great at your audition yesterday. Brittany told me you were amazing!"

We were driving in our Mustang on Tuesday afternoon, headed for KWOW. We had a special package to deliver to Wild Will.

Mary-Kate had been down ever since the audition. But I could tell it didn't have anything to do with her performance. It was more about Jake. But every time I asked her about him, she changed the subject.

"They're announcing the cast tomorrow," Mary-Kate told me. "I guess we'll know how I did then."

I put on my left blinker and pulled onto the highway. Mary-Kate grabbed our package from the backseat.

"This *has* to get Wild Will's attention!" I said, nodding at the box in her hands.

We'd wrapped up a copy of Sweetbriar's CD, *Starring You and Me,* in colorful paper. Then we tied a million different colored balloons to it.

We'd also attached a letter explaining all about Brian and Penny and the free concert at the school. The letter invited Wild Will to the concert to hear Brian and Penny live.

Our plan was to hand the package to Wild Will and give him our speech about what great musicians Brian and Penny were.

I slipped my own copy of *Starring You and Me* into the CD player and cranked the volume up.

"Has Brian called you back yet?" Mary-Kate asked.

"No," I admitted. "It's been a few days now. But I'm not worried. He's probably just dealing with rehearsals and stuff. I mean, it's his career on the line!"

"Talk about pressure," Mary-Kate agreed.

She tapped the package with her fingers. "Don't worry, Ash. Our plan will work. I just know it."

I nodded. "You're right. Besides, it has to."

I turned up the volume on the car stereo a couple of more notches. Mary-Kate and I both sang along to the CD for a few minutes.

"So, what about Jake?" I asked. "Have you talked to him since yesterday?"

Mary-Kate sighed. "No. I feel like too much of a jerk," she admitted. "He was trying to be sweet by auditioning for the play, and I totally blew up at him."

I wanted to help Mary-Kate. But I'd have to do that later. Right now I had to concentrate on getting Wild Will to Brian and Penny's concert!

KWOW's building loomed ahead of us. "Here we are," I said, pulling into the parking lot.

We headed inside the building and approached the guard at the front desk. "We have a package for Wild Will," Mary-Kate said.

"Leave the package here," the guard instructed.

"Oh, no," I chimed in. "This is a personal item. We were instructed to leave the package upstairs."

"Is anyone up there expecting this?" the guard asked, eyeing our balloons suspiciously.

I glanced at Mary-Kate. I didn't like to lie, but it was for Brian's sake. "Sure," I said. "We spoke to his assistant, Peter. He told us to come right up."

The guard glanced down at his desk. "Take the elevator to your right," he instructed. "Twenty-first floor."

"Thanks!" I cried. We hurried to the elevator.

"I can't believe it!" Mary-Kate whispered. "We're in!"

We rode the elevator to the twenty-first floor.

The doors slid open, and a stern-looking receptionist glared at us.

"May I help you?" the receptionist asked.

"Yes," I said. "We're here to see Wild Will."

"Just a moment, please." The receptionist picked up the phone and dialed a number. "Someone here for Will," she announced. Then she hung up.

"You can wait here," she told us.

My heart thumped against my rib cage. Wild Will was on his way out of his office—to talk to *us*! Could it really be this easy?

A thin young man with messy black hair appeared. "Yes?" he asked.

I blinked. "Um, are you—Wild Will?" I asked.

"No, I'm Peter, Will's assistant," the young man said.

"Oh. Well, can we please talk to Wild Will?"

"He's in a meeting," Peter stated. "Can I ask who you are and why you're here?"

I sighed. "My name is Ashley—"

"Hey!" Peter interrupted. "Fan-club girl! Nice to see you!" He turned to Mary-Kate. "I guess this is your sister."

Mary-Kate nodded and shook Peter's hand.

"Well, you guys can give me whatever message you have for Will," Peter told us. "I'll make sure he gets it."

Mary-Kate and I exchanged looks. What could we do? Right now, this was as far as we were going to get.

Mary-Kate handed the package to Peter. "We brought this CD for him," she explained. "It's very important that he listen to it—and read the letter attached."

Peter took the package. "Sure, no problem," he said. "Thanks, girls."

He turned and started back inside the office.

Maybe this will be okay, I thought. As long as Wild Will got the package, what did it matter *who* handed it to him? It was so colorfully decorated and irresistible-looking that Wild Will was sure to want to know what it was. Right?

Wrong.

Peter stopped and set the package on a table behind the receptionist's desk. I had to stand on tiptoe to see what was on the table.

My heart sank when I spied dozens of other CD-shaped packages, one more colorfully decorated than the next! All had envelopes attached. And I had a feeling that they were all addressed to Wild Will.

I turned to Mary-Kate. "Looks like we'd better come up with a new plan—and fast! The concert is only three days away!"

I pushed through the glass doors and entered the lobby of Brian and Penny's hotel.

After our latest defeat at Wild Will's radio station, I thought I could use some cheering up. So I dropped Mary-Kate off at home and decided to pay Brian a surprise visit.

Not only did I need a laugh, I wanted to make sure Brian was okay.

Several days without talking did make me a little worried, and once I saw that Brian was fine, I'd be able to concentrate on a new idea to get Wild Will's attention.

I removed my sunglasses and blinked. It always took a moment for my eyes to adjust from the bright Los Angeles sunshine, to the dimness of the indoors.

"Hi, Ashley!" I turned toward the voice.

Penny waved to me from an overstuffed armchair. A music magazine sat open on her lap. I smiled and went over to her.

"Hey, how's it going, Penny?" I asked, flopping down in a chair next to her.

"Great," she said. "Thanks to you and Mary-Kate. Brian and I are totally excited about the concert!"

"So Brian's okay, right?" I asked.

Penny looked at me quizzically. "Yeah, why wouldn't he be?"

"It's just that I haven't heard from him in a few days, and I was worried," I said.

"Oh, well, he's all wrapped up in planning the concert," Penny explained. "It's so incredible that the hottest DJ in town is going to mention it on the radio—and then actually introduce us before we go onstage!"

I swallowed hard. It *would* be incredible—when

we finally got Wild Will to do it!

"Ummm—do you know if Brian's in his room?" I asked.

"I think he is." Penny glanced at me. Her expression grew concerned. "Ashley, is something wrong?"

"Well, I don't know," I answered honestly. "I had a really great date with Brian a few nights ago. That's why I'm surprised I haven't heard from him since."

"What do you mean, you had a date with Brian?" Penny asked.

"Um, you know, a date," I said, confused by her question. "He took me out. We walked on the beach."

Penny frowned. "Are you sure it was a *date* date?"

"Positive," I said. "Why?"

She bit her lip. "Ash, there's something you should know. I think you'd better talk to Brian."

"Hello, Brian?" I called. "It's me, Ashley."

I knocked on the door to Brian's room again, but there was no answer.

I was on my way back through the lobby, when I noticed someone by the pool.

Brian!

As I walked out through the glass doors that led

to the pool area, I couldn't stop thinking about what Penny said.

Are you sure it was a date *date? There's something you should know. You'd better talk to Brian. . . .*

What did that mean? Of course our date the other night had been a *date* date. After all, hadn't he been the one to suggest the moonlit walk on the beach? And hadn't he been the one to lean down and kiss me?

There was no doubt in my mind. It had definitely been a date!

The sun was hot on my shoulders as I stepped out onto the patio. Brian was standing by a bunch of empty lounge chairs. He had his back to me.

What I really wanted was to sneak up behind him and put my arms around him. But now I was so confused by what Penny had said, I decided against it.

I headed over and was about to call Brian's name, when I realized he was on his cell phone.

"I really miss you, too, Cara," he said into the phone.

I froze.

Cara? Who was that?

Brian had never mentioned a Cara before.

"I wish you could be here, too, sweetie," Brian continued.

Sweetie? I thought.

"I'm not sure when I'll be home," Brian said. "It depends on what happens with the concert."

I felt terrible for eavesdropping, but I couldn't move. *Who was Cara?*

Brian laughed. "Of *course* we'll still be together when I'm rich and famous."

I felt as though someone had punched me in the stomach. I could not believe what I was hearing.

I wrapped my arms around myself—a shiver ran through my body.

After I decided to trust Brian. After I told him exactly what I was feeling—I had finally learned the truth.

Brian had a girlfriend!

chapter twelve

"**I** can't wait to get back home to see you, Cara," Brian said into his cell phone.

I clutched my stomach and struggled to breathe. Why hadn't he told me about Cara?

I started to back away.

Don't turn around, I silently willed him. I didn't want him to see me.

Why did he do it? I wondered. Why did he chase after me if he had a girlfriend?

Anger, embarrassment, confusion, and hurt all mixed together. I wanted to take his phone and throw it in the pool! But I controlled myself. I continued toward the patio door. Then—

Screeeee! I bumped right into a lounge chair. It scraped against the concrete on the deck. Brian whipped around.

Oh, no.

We locked gazes. I could feel my face turn

bright red. Brian's, on the other hand, turned white.

He looked away for a moment. "Um, Cara," he said into the phone, "can I call you back a little later? Something important has come up."

I just stood there, fuming.

"Uh, me, too," he said. Then he clicked off the phone and put it in his pocket.

"Ashley, I—" he began.

"Why didn't you tell me that you had a girlfriend?" I interrupted.

Brian looked really upset. "I'm sorry, Ashley. I tried to tell you."

My eyes widened. "Oh, really?" I said sarcastically. "When? Because I don't remember that at all. I remember you saying you wanted to get back together with me. I remember you *kissing* me. But a girlfriend? No. You never mentioned that."

"I *wanted* to tell you," he insisted.

"So, why didn't you?" I demanded.

He looked at the pool, then back at me. "I like you so much, Ashley. I didn't want to tell you because maybe I kind of didn't want it to be true."

"Didn't want *what* to be true?" I asked. "How much you like me or that you have a girlfriend?"

He paused.

"When I saw you again, it all came back to me," he explained. "How amazing things were between us. I guess part of me wanted it to be that way again."

He ran his hand through his thick brown hair. "And then you were so incredible—helping us out, just the way you did over the summer. You were doing so much for us. How could I tell you that . . . that I had moved on."

I stood there totally speechless. What a slime!

I couldn't help but wonder—did he ever really want me to be his girlfriend—or did he just want me to help save his career?

"Ashley, I wasn't lying when I said I never stopped thinking about you," Brian continued. "And I do wish we could be together. It's just—I'm so far away. And things are different now."

I felt my throat close up. "Well, you should have told me that you 'moved on' *before* you asked me out on a date," I said. "And you shouldn't have kissed me."

He looked upset. "I know. But I was just so confused. I'm sorry for leading you on."

"I'm sorry, too, Brian," I said. "Sorry I misjudged you. I thought you were a nice guy—and that you would be a great boyfriend. I guess I was wrong."

❀

As I headed for my bedroom, I heard one of the tracks from *Starring You and Me* coming from Ashley's room.

It was "Blue Eyes," the song Brian wrote for her.

"Until I saw your face, I never knew . . .
That a girl could mean so much to me."

I peered in. Ashley was lying on her bed, staring up at the ceiling. The track ended and started again. Ashley had the CD player on repeat.

Uh-oh. This did not look good.

I knocked softly on her door. "Ashley?" I called. "What's wrong?"

She turned toward me. Her eyes were red rimmed, and her face was streaked with tears.

"Oh, nothing," she told me. "Just that Brian has a girlfriend in Seattle."

"What?" I gasped. I sat down next to her. "But that doesn't make sense. He's been flirting with you since the first day we saw him! How could he have a girlfriend?"

Ashley shrugged and rolled onto her side. "I heard him talking to her on his cell phone. He was keeping it a secret from me. I was never supposed to find out about it."

She glanced at her stereo and frowned. "Do me a favor, Mary-Kate. Turn off the CD player. I don't even know why I'm listening to it."

I switched off the stereo.

"I thought we had something really special," she said. "But now I don't know. Did he *ever* really care about me? Or was he just lying the whole time?"

"Ashley, I know he cared about you," I told her. "I think he still does."

"Well, I don't care about him," she said. "And he can forget about me helping his career. I'm not trying to get Wild Will's attention for Brian and Penny's CD anymore."

I frowned. "Wait a second, Ashley. Brian acted like a jerk. But that doesn't really have anything to do with the concert—or getting Wild Will to advertise it."

"Of course it does. Why should I help Brian after what he did to me?" she asked.

I placed a hand on her shoulder. "I know you're hurt," I said. "I would be, too. But you don't really want to ruin Brian and Penny's career, do you?"

Ashley rolled over and put her pillow over her head. "Their whole stupid concert can be canceled for all I care," she mumbled.

chapter thirteen

Mr. Owen took center stage as everyone filed into the auditorium.

This was it. Wednesday afternoon. The moment I'd been waiting for.

Everyone started buzzing as Mr. Owen cleared his throat and held up a sheaf of papers.

"As soon as you're all seated, I'd like to announce the cast for the fall production of *Grease*!"

My palms were sweating. My heart was racing. I couldn't take the suspense!

"You totally got Sandy," Brittany whispered from her seat next to me. "Your audition was awesome."

"Thanks," I said. "And you are definitely a Pink Lady. We're going to have a blast rehearsing together."

We huddled close together as we waited for Mr.

Owen to begin. Even if I didn't win the role of Sandy, I hoped I'd get a decent part. Maybe Rizzo, the leader of the Pink Ladies, or Frenchy, one of my favorite characters.

But the truth was, I wanted Sandy very badly. I'd worked so hard for it. I just had to hope my luck would change.

So far today, things hadn't exactly gone my way. I couldn't convince Ashley not to give up on Brian and Penny's concert. And I couldn't reach Jake.

I tried calling him the night before, but he was out with friends. Then today he had a team meeting at lunch. I had the feeling he was avoiding me in the hallways between periods.

I'd given a lot of thought to what he said about our relationship. He was right. I had been acting kind of selfishly.

I accused him of not respecting the fact that drama was important to me. But hadn't he given up a whole lunch period to help me put up flyers?

I should have set some time aside for him. I should have shown him that drama club wasn't the only thing that was important to me. He was important, too.

I peered over at Danielle. She was flipping through a textbook on her lap, pretending she didn't care that parts were about to be announced.

Figures, I thought. *Ms. I'm-So-Cool strikes again.*

"Okay, everyone," Mr. Owen said. "I'm going to start with the chorus and then work my way up to the lead roles."

Great! Now I'd be bursting with suspense till the very end! Mr. Owen sure had a flair for the dramatic.

As Mr. Owen read down the list, I clapped for all the people who got roles. Brittany and I hugged when she was chosen as a Pink Lady.

Then it was time for the leads—finally!

"The part of Danny Zuko will be played by Nathan Sparks," Mr. Owen said. "But I did appreciate Jake Impenna's audition. He was a very good sport."

The crowd laughed, remembering Jake's display. To my surprise, I found myself smiling. It *was* kind of funny, when I looked back on it.

"And finally," Mr. Owen said, "the role of Sandy." He put down the sheaf of papers and faced the audience.

I peeked at Danielle. For the first time, she looked a little nervous.

Brittany squeezed my hand.

"We had a very hard time deciding who should get this role," Mr. Owen said. "Two of our Sandy contenders were very strong."

Danielle and I glanced each other, then looked back at Mr. Owen.

"Thanks to Mary-Kate Olsen," he continued,

"we're able to put on this production of *Grease* in the first place. Her tireless effort at recruiting new members deserves a special round of applause."

Everyone clapped. Normally, I'd feel really good about being singled out that way. But at the moment, the anticipation was killing me. *Who* got the part?

"Therefore," Mr. Owen continued, "the judges have decided to award the role of Sandy to Mary-Kate! Our runner-up, Danielle, has been given the part of Rizzo—an excellent role that will certainly make use of her considerable talent."

Danielle gasped. I turned to give her a triumphant smile. But when I saw the look on her face, I stopped.

Then she ran out of the auditorium, leaving her textbook and backpack on the seat beside her.

Everyone else in the room cheered wildly. But instead of feeling victorious, I just felt funny.

I had won. I was Sandy.

So why did I suddenly feel bad for Danielle?

R-ring!

I snatched up the phone, hoping it was Mary-Kate calling with good news about the *Grease* announcements.

"Hello?" I answered.

"Hi," the voice on the line responded. "It's Penny."

"Oh." I slumped down on my bed, disappointed.

"I'm just calling to see how you're doing," Penny continued. "I hope you don't mind, but Brian told me the whole story last night. I know that you must be feeling hurt."

I didn't say anything. For one thing, I had a tremendous lump in my throat. For another, I felt totally confused.

"Look, Ashley, I know this is none of my business, but I consider you both really good friends of mine. I feel like I have to say *something*," Penny declared.

"I'm listening," I said.

I heard her let out a sigh. She sounded relieved.

It was nice to know that Penny cared, but I couldn't imagine anything she could say that could make the situation between Brian and me okay again.

"Brian feels very bad about what he did," Penny began. "He realizes that he was wrong not to tell you about Cara right away."

"Well, he's right about that," I said.

"He really wants to explain himself to you," Penny said, "better than he did out by the pool."

"I don't know," I told her. "He explained himself just fine. What more is there to say?"

"A lot," Penny insisted. "He wants to make everything up to you, but he's afraid that you don't want to speak to him."

"Well, he's right about that, too," I said. "I *don't* want to speak to him. Ever again."

There was a long pause.

"Look, Ashley, I don't know if this will help or not, but I think you should know just how wild and confusing the past couple of months have been for Brian and me."

"What do you mean?" I asked.

"I mean, it's amazing that Brian and I even know our own names after all that's happened to us," she explained. "First we got the recording contract, and the future seemed totally bright. Then we worked like crazy recording the CD—making sure it was perfect. Making sure it was something that people would love. But it's not selling. And now, we're scared to death of being dropped by the record label."

She paused and took a deep breath. "All we ever wanted was to play music," she continued. "It's our dream! But during the past month, we've both felt like someone dangled the dream in front of us, only to take it away."

I thought about everything Penny said. Things must have been really rough. Exciting one minute— and then scary and horrible the next.

Could I really blame Brian for acting so weirdly? I stared down at the pattern on my bedspread. How would I have acted, I wondered, if I were in his situation?

"What Brian did was wrong," Penny said. "I'm angry about it, too, and I told him so. I only wish I could have figured out what was going on sooner. Then, maybe, I could have stopped the whole thing from happening."

"Thanks," I said. "I really appreciate that."

I stared up at the ceiling—and a thought occurred to me. Even if Brian didn't deserve my help, *Penny* was a good friend. I wanted her to succeed. I couldn't just let her dream die—not when she'd come so far.

I stood and walked over to my desk. "You know what, Penny? I'm really glad you called. Don't worry about the record company. Your concert is going to turn things around for you and Brian. You'll see. Everything's going to work out."

"I sure hope so," Penny answered, "and I really hope you'll give Brian a chance to talk to you."

I still didn't know about that.

But I was back on a mission—ready to make Sweetbriar one of the best-selling groups ever!

chapter fourteen

After Danielle ran out of the auditorium, I picked up her book and her backpack. And when the meeting was over, I got into my car and drove straight to her house.

Danielle had been totally mean to me, but for some reason, I had to find out if she was okay.

I parked and ran up the walk to her front door. I pressed the buzzer and waited.

No answer.

I pressed the buzzer again, and knocked loudly for good measure.

Still nothing.

I put the backpack on the front step and headed back to my car.

Then, out of the corner of my eye, I caught a flash of strawberry-blond hair. Danielle was sitting on a bench around the side of her house.

"Danielle?" I asked softly.

She glanced up at me. "What are you doing here?" she snapped.

"You left your backpack," I explained. "And besides, I wanted to talk to you about what happened."

"There's nothing to talk about," Danielle said. "You won. And there's no way I'm taking a lesser role than the lead. I'm quitting the play."

"What? Why?" I asked. "You're such a good actress—and the play really needs you. You'll make an amazing Rizzo!"

Danielle burst into tears.

"Danielle, what is so terrible about getting the supporting role?" I asked. "Rizzo is a huge part—almost as big as Sandy."

Danielle swiped a hand over her eyes. "You don't understand," she said, her voice trembling. "My mother is one of the most famous actresses in Hollywood. She doesn't audition for roles—she just gets them. She expects the same from me."

"But your mom didn't start out getting offered the leads," I reasoned. "She worked her way up to where she is now."

"That doesn't matter," Danielle insisted. "I'm supposed to be *better* than she is. She keeps telling me how lucky I am. That I have all the advantages she never did. The best acting classes. My own voice coach. Not to mention advice from a great actress—

my own mother!" She sniffled. "I can't be second-best. My mother won't let me!"

"So if your mom found out that you lost the lead . . ." I started.

". . . she'd have a fit," Danielle finished. "Last year, I was in summer stock. I loved it because my mother wasn't there. But then she came to see the play, and she cut my performance to shreds. She expects me to be flawless—*all* the time."

Wow, I thought. I couldn't even imagine the kind of pressure Danielle was under. I'd always spurred *myself* on to do my best. But even if I blew it, I knew I had the support of my family and friends to fall back on.

Danielle reached into her pocket for a tissue and blew her nose. "So, after a while I decided that I wanted nothing more to do with acting. My mother was just too intense—and I didn't want to have to deal with it."

"So that's why you didn't sign up for the drama club," I realized.

Danielle nodded. "When school started, my mom asked me if I joined, and I told her there *wasn't* a drama club. But then you showed up at my house with your stupid flyer. My mother *insisted* that I audition."

"Did you tell her you didn't want to?" I asked.

Danielle snorted. "Of course I did. Three times. But she didn't care. She said it would be 'just adorable' for me to play Sandy in my high school production of *Grease*. When she finds out I didn't get the part, she'll never let me live it down."

Now it all made sense. Why Danielle was rude to me when I asked her to be in the play. Why she had gone after my role—at least, the role that I thought belonged to me—and why she'd been so intense about it.

Her mom forced her into it. And, in a way, so did I. But something that she said made me feel like maybe—just maybe—all of this could be okay.

"Danielle," I began. "I don't think you tried out for *Grease* because of your mom."

"Ha! What do you know?" she mumbled through her tissue.

"You did it because you love acting," I said. "You were having a ball on that stage during auditions. I could tell. And you were good. Really good."

"So?" Danielle asked.

"So why don't you do the play just for fun?" I answered. "Who cares what your mom thinks! Rizzo is a great role. Take it! Take it because *you* want it."

Danielle looked up, sniffling. "You know, the funny thing is, I always wanted to play Rizzo. She's really rough around the edges. And Sandy is such a goody-goody."

I laughed. "Think about it, Danielle. We could have a blast at rehearsals. And the play will be a huge hit!"

Danielle sighed. "Okay, Mary-Kate," she said. "I'll think about it."

✤

"Think, Mary-Kate. Think!" I said, panic rising in my voice. "The concert is *tomorrow*. What are we going to do?"

"I don't know!" Mary-Kate answered. "Just give me a few minutes to come up with something."

It was Thursday morning, and Mary-Kate and I had been excused from classes to help prepare for Brian and Penny's concert.

It was a good thing. We needed all the time we could get! If Wild Will didn't announce the concert on his show—and introduce the show himself— then Brian and Penny could kiss their musical careers good-bye!

Mary-Kate leaned against the pillows on her bed and closed her eyes. We were listening to Wild Will's radio show, trying desperately to come up with a last-minute answer to our problem.

Wild Will took a station break, and some commercials followed. The last one was for Clementine's Café.

"Yeah, Clementine's Café," Will said when he returned to the air. "Love that joint. I get my lunch from there every day."

"I know," his producer, a woman named Barbara, commented. "Smoked turkey and Swiss cheese on rye with mustard. You've ordered the same lunch, from the same place, every day for the last five years. Don't you ever get sick of it?"

"Why should I?" Wild Will asked. "Clementine's rocks. And speaking of rockin', check out this new song from Smudge—on KWOW, Los Angeles's hottest hit music station!"

The song came on. But I barely heard the lyrics. Something was tickling my brain—the beginning of an idea.

"Mary-Kate," I cried. "I've got it! I know how we can get in to see Wild Will—and he definitely won't turn us away!"

chapter fifteen

Mary-Kate and I entered the front door of Clementine's Café at eleven-thirty that morning. There was plenty of time before lunch.

I filled Mary-Kate in on my plan during the car ride there. It was a long shot, Mary-Kate agreed. But this was our last chance. It *had* to work.

"Hi," I said to the woman behind the take-out counter. "Smoked turkey and Swiss cheese on rye bread with mustard, please."

"Sounds like you're ordering for Wild Will," the woman said. "You two must be new at the station. I don't think I've seen you in here before."

"Ummm—right! We're new interns at KWOW," Mary-Kate told her. "Wild Will's assistant asked us to pick up his lunch today."

"Coming right up, girls," she said, and turned around to make the sandwich.

We took a seat on a padded bench. Mary-Kate

nudged me in the ribs and gestured at the wall above the cash register. A Clementine's Café baseball cap and T-shirt were tacked up there. A sign beside them read: FOR SALE.

The woman turned back around and wrapped up Wild Will's sandwich.

"Anything else, girls?" she asked.

"We'll take two of those Clementine T-shirts," Mary-Kate said. "And two baseball caps."

"Good thinking," I whispered while the woman went to the back to find our size. "The caps will hide our faces—so Peter and the receptionist won't recognize us."

"Exactly," Mary-Kate said. "And we'll look like official delivery people—so no one will try to stop us!"

Five minutes later, we were back in our car with Wild Will's lunch. We pulled on our new Clementine's T-shirts over our tank tops. Then we tucked our hair into the caps. Finally, we slipped Brian and Penny's CD inside the lunch bag.

"This is going to work!" Mary-Kate shouted. "We definitely look like Clementine delivery girls!"

"Yes!" We high-fived the way we used to when we were little. We drove to the station, blasting *Starring You and Me* to get us really revved up. We pulled into the lot and giggled when we saw the accountant's cherry red sports car. He'd probably listened to Brian and Penny's CD on his way to work that morning!

At the front desk, the security guard glanced at our T-shirts and didn't say a word—he just waved us right by to the elevator!

At the twenty-first floor, the elevator pinged open. *Here goes nothing,* I thought. We stepped out of the elevator, and the receptionist glanced up at us.

I pulled the bill of my cap down low over my face. I was about to say something, but the receptionist beat me to it.

"You're a little early, but go on in," she said.

We walked past her, and found ourselves wandering the halls of the radio station!

We looked at every nameplate on every office door, searching for Wild Will's name. Nothing so far.

"Hey, look!" Mary-Kate whispered. She pointed at a huge poster on the wall. It featured an attractive, shaggy-haired, thirty-something man in a black T-shirt and a huge smile. A line underneath read, *WILD WILL WITHERS, LOS ANGELES'S HOTTEST MORNING DJ!*

I glanced down toward the end of the hall—and gasped.

"There he is!" I cried. "Up ahead, through those glass doors."

Mary-Kate and I could see Wild Will sitting in an office by himself.

"Let's go!" I said. We jogged down the hall and burst into the room before anyone could stop us.

"Wild Will!" I cried. "You have to hear this CD. It's by this group called Sweetbriar—and they're totally awesome." I pulled the CD out of the lunch bag and dropped it on the desk.

"They're having a free concert tomorrow night at eight," Mary-Kate chimed in. "It's at our school, Malibu High, and once you hear their CD, you'll totally want to be there to introduce them and—"

A movement in the corner of my field of vision caught my attention. A man behind another large window was frowning deeply, waving frantically, and pointing to a red, blinking ON THE AIR sign.

Oh, no! We'd walked right into the middle of Wild Will's show!

Wild Will turned and stared. But before he could say a word, two beefy security guards burst into the room and grabbed us.

"Hey—watch it!" Mary-Kate cried. She dropped the lunch bag as they dragged us out of the room.

"We can walk ourselves out, you know," I said. But the guards wouldn't let go of us until we were outside the building.

"We don't want to see you girls at this station again," one of the security guards barked. "Do I make myself clear?"

113

We nodded, and the men stomped back inside the building.

We trudged back to our car, totally defeated.

"We're doomed!" I wailed. "There's no way Wild Will will be at the concert now. Brian and Penny's career is ruined."

Mary-Kate sighed. "I was so sure that our plan was going to work."

We climbed into the Mustang and turned on the radio. Wild Will's voice filled the car.

"Change the station, Mary-Kate," I said. "I can't listen to it. It's too depressing."

Mary-Kate reached out to turn the knob, but just then Wild Will mentioned Sweetbriar!

"So many people have been calling in after hearing those two girls on the air," the DJ said. "Everyone wants to know who Sweetbriar is. So I've decided to play a track from the CD. I haven't heard this yet, so hold on tight, because here it is, everyone!"

Our mouths fell open. Brian and Penny's voices poured over the radio's speakers!

We might not have been able to get Wild Will to advertise the concert or attend it, but we did manage to get Brian and Penny's song on the radio.

Mary-Kate grinned at me. "They sound great, don't they?"

I nodded. "Yeah. I just wish we could have

gotten Wild Will to come to the concert."

"What do you think Mr. McKenna is going to say when he doesn't show up?" Mary-Kate asked. "Do you think he'll drop Brian and Penny from his record company?"

"I don't know," I told her. "I just don't know."

chapter sixteen

"It's two-thirty, Mary-Kate," Ashley reminded me. "Don't you have to get to rehearsal?"

"Oh yeah—thanks," I said. I jumped off her bed. After the fiasco at KWOW, we'd spent the afternoon making sure everything would be ready for the concert the next day.

Now I had to get to school. The new cast of *Grease* was meeting for our first read-through.

I had something else to take care of, too— something even more important. Jake's baseball team, the Malibu High Tigers, had a game that afternoon against Westwood High, our biggest rivals. And I had a plan to show him how much he mattered to me.

"Will you be okay here?" I asked.

Ashley nodded. "Everything is under control. Have a good rehearsal! And go, Tigers!"

"Thanks!" I hurried off to school. I was running

late, so I jogged from the parking lot to the auditorium. Everyone with a speaking part in the show had gathered around a long table, headed by Mr. Owen. I took an empty seat next to him. Nathan sat across the table from me. There was an empty chair beside me—the last seat left.

Danielle, I thought, my heart sinking. *She's not here. I really thought she'd change her mind.*

"Well, looks like everyone's arrived," Mr. Owen said. "Except, of course, our Rizzo. We'll give her a few more minutes."

"Wait," a voice called from the doorway. "I need a moment to prepare."

All eyes turned toward the door. Danielle breezed in, script in hand, making a dramatic entrance, as usual.

She took the empty seat and glanced at me out of the corner of her eye. Her lips broke into a teeny-tiny grin.

Mr. Owen beamed. "Ms. Bloom, I'm very glad to see you. Very glad. People, I think we've got a hit on our hands. Now let's get to work."

"Great job, people," Mr. Owen said after the read-through. "A promising first read. Now I'll need to break you up into groups to work on specific parts of the script. Mary-Kate, I'd like you to work with Danielle this afternoon."

This afternoon? I thought. *Meaning right now?*

Jake's baseball game was just about to start. I wasn't used to saying no when the drama club needed me. But this time I had to. I just had to.

"Mr. Owen," I began. "I'm afraid I have to leave."

Mr. Owen blinked at me through his rimless glasses. "Leave? But you have the lead role, Mary-Kate," he said. "You can't miss rehearsals—your part is too important."

"But there's something else I have to do now," I told him. "It's important, too."

"Mary-Kate—" Mr. Owen began. "I—"

"It's okay, Mr. Owen," Danielle cut in. "Mary-Kate can come to my house over the weekend. We'll make up the rehearsal time."

I stared at Danielle, amazed and grateful.

"All right," Mr. Owen agreed. "Just don't fall behind. I'd like both of you to know a good portion of your lines by next week."

"Don't worry, Mr. Owen, we will," I promised. "And thanks," I whispered to Danielle. "I owe you one."

"No problem," she said. "My mom is having a party this weekend. She wanted to have the house all to herself. Too bad she's going to have to make some room for us!"

I laughed as I stuffed my script in my backpack.

I slung it over my shoulder and hurried to the baseball field.

Jake and his teammates had just finished their warm-up. They ran onto the field and took their positions to start the first inning. Jake punched his glove and crouched down, ready to play.

The bleachers were crowded. I found a seat in the top row and settled in next to a row of guys. The one nearest to me had fuzzy blond hair.

"Let's go, Tigers!" the guys shouted. "Let's go!"

"I guess you're baseball fans," I said, making conversation.

"Yup. And this is a huge game for us," the blond guy confided. "Westwood has beaten Malibu the last three years in a row. But if we can beat them this year, we have a shot at the championship."

"Maybe this'll help," I said. I opened my backpack and pulled out five sheets of oak tag. "Will you pass these down to your friends?"

"Cool," the blond guy said.

When everyone had their signs, I gave the signal. We stood up, holding the signs over our heads. I had printed a message on them the night before. It read: THE TIGERS ARE IMPENNA-TRABLE! GO TIGERS!

It was a goofy pun, but I couldn't resist.

I cheered and whistled loudly. A minute or two

later, a couple of the players noticed it. They started clapping and pointing at the banner.

People in the bleachers turned around to read it. "Yeah!" they shouted, clapping and whistling. "Go, Tigers!"

Jake waved to me from the field, grinning like crazy. I flipped my piece of oak tag—the last one in the message—around. On the reverse side, I had printed I LOVE YOU, JAKE!

"Go, Jake!" I shouted. "Go, Tigers!"

"Go, Mary-Kate!" Jake shouted back. "You're the best!"

chapter seventeen

The crowd roared with excitement.

"Oh my gosh! Look at all the people out there!" I gasped.

Friday had come at last, and Brian and Penny's show was starting in about twenty minutes. A stage had been set up at one end of the baseball field. Ashley and I stood backstage while workers set up the equipment.

Out front, people were pouring onto the field. The bleachers were already full and the field was so packed, you couldn't see a patch of grass.

Ashley bounced up and down with excitement. "We did it, Mary-Kate!" she cried. "Can you believe it?"

I chuckled. "Truthfully? No. I can't believe it."

"Oh! There you are, girls." Mr. McKenna, the record company executive, approached us. A couple of people with press passes around their necks trailed behind him.

"You two did a great job," Mr. McKenna told us. "I can't believe the buzz this concert is getting! The station manager at KWOW told me that since you pulled your on-air stunt they've had hundreds of requests for songs from *Starring You and Me*. I've been fielding calls from magazines and newspapers all morning. Everyone wants interviews with Brian and Penny! It's been crazy! Not that I mind."

"So—have you changed your mind about dropping Brian and Penny from your label?" Ashley asked.

"Are you kidding?" Mr. McKenna said. "Brian and Penny are our hottest new act! I'm going to sign them to a three-year deal!"

Ashley squeezed my hand. "Excellent!" she said.

"Mary-Kate!" Jake shouted over the noise. He'd managed to work his way up to the front of the field, right next to the stage.

"Mary-Kate!" he repeated.

I hurried over to him, and hopped off the stage right into his arms.

We had made up the day before, right after the Tigers won the game. It was as if we had never even fought.

"Hey, look!" Jake said, pointing to a blanket on the grass. "I found us a great spot for the concert." He paused and stared into my eyes. "A great spot for the greatest girl."

He leaned close and kissed me. I felt warm all over. I was so glad to have him back!

"I guess the show will be starting soon," he said. "Want to stretch out on the blanket?"

"Hey, I'm with the band," I said. "I can get us backstage!"

Jake laughed and packed up his blanket. "What are we waiting for? Let's go!"

❀

"I'm sorry that I didn't tell you about Cara right away, Ashley," Brian said to me. "I was wrong. Really wrong."

Brian and Penny were standing backstage, waiting to go on. As soon as he had seen me, Brian pulled me aside and tried to explain himself.

He wants me to let him off the hook, I realized. *He's about to give the biggest concert of his career, and he doesn't want to feel guilty about what he did.*

"You *were* wrong, Brian," I said. "You really hurt me."

He stared at his feet. "It was just that—"

"Forget it," I interrupted. "I already have. I think we both just need to move on."

"Five minutes till show time!" Mr. McKenna called out. "Are you guys ready?"

"Ready," Brian said. He picked up his guitar. Then he and I joined Penny, Jake, and Mary-Kate. "We owe you guys so much!" Penny said.

"It's true—we can't thank you enough," Brian added.

"No problem," Mary-Kate said. "We'll take a free concert as payment."

Brian and Penny laughed.

"Brian!" someone called.

We turned and saw a red-haired girl rushing toward us.

"Cara!" Brian exclaimed.

So that's Brian's girlfriend, I thought. Her long hair shone in the stage lights. I noticed a smattering of freckles running across her nose.

She leaped into Brian's arms.

"What are you doing here?" Brian asked. He looked totally surprised.

"My parents let me fly to Los Angeles for your first concert," Cara said. "Isn't that cool? My mom's sitting in the front row!"

"Awesome!" Brian said. "I'm so happy that you're here!"

My stomach tightened as I watched Brian with his girlfriend.

"Cara, there's someone I want you to meet," Brian said. He turned to me. "This is Ashley, the girl I was telling you about."

"Hi, Ashley," Cara said. "Brian told me how much you've done for him and Penny. I'm so glad he has a friend like you."

"Thanks," I said. I had to admit that she seemed very sweet.

"Okay, you two," Mr. Needham, the principal, told Brian and Penny, "It's time to take the stage!"

"Not just yet, it isn't," a male voice said.

We all turned around. I blinked at the sight of a tall man with shaggy brown hair.

Wild Will!

"Wow," Mary-Kate gasped. "It's really you! I can't believe you're here!"

"Hey, it's the delivery girls!" Wild Will said. "I thought you might be here."

We both turned red with embarrassment.

"Ummm—I'm Ashley," I said, "and this is my sister, Mary-Kate."

"Sorry about the way we barged in on your show," Mary-Kate apologized. "We had no idea you were on the air."

"That's all right," Wild Will said. "In fact, my fans loved it! I think it made the show even zanier. But next time you want to make an appearance, give me a call first. Okay?"

Mary-Kate and I grinned. "You've got it!"

Wild Will turned to Brian and Penny. "Your friends asked me to introduce your concert," he said. "And I love your CD so much, I couldn't pass up the chance."

"Really?" Penny gasped.

"That would be awesome!" Brian said.

"But I need a favor from you," Wild Will added. "I'd like to book you as guests on my morning show."

"Sure!" Penny cried. "We'd love it!" She and Brian looked as if they were going to explode from excitement.

At that moment, Mom and Dad walked backstage. They'd saved seats on the field and were going to have a picnic during the concert.

"Hi, girls," Dad said. He gave us both a hug. "This is turning into quite a show. I'm so proud of you both!"

Then he looked up. "Hey! Wild Will!" he said. "I'm not surprised to see you here. Brian and Penny are quite a talent. Even if they are with another label."

Wild Will laughed and shook Dad's hand. "Mark! What brings you here? Scoping out the competition?"

Dad shook his head. "My wife and I are here with our daughters. And their friends." He put one arm around me, and other around Mary-Kate.

Wild Will stared at us, totally surprised. "These are your daughters?"

Dad nodded. "Yes. This is Mary-Kate, and this is Ashley."

"I know," Wild Will said. "We've already met."

Then he leaned toward us. "Why didn't you tell

me who your dad was?" he whispered. "You didn't have to dress up like delivery girls to get me to listen to a CD. All you had to do was tell my assistant who you were!"

"Really?" Mary-Kate yelped. "You mean we hid behind cars, disguised ourselves, and acted like total idiots for nothing?"

"Well, not exactly nothing," I put in. "We made this happen on our own, Mary-Kate. Because we worked hard, not because we knew the right people."

"Yeah," Mary-Kate agreed. "I guess that is kind of impressive."

"I know *I'm* impressed," Wild Will said. "Well, I've got a concert to introduce. See you later!"

Wild Will ran onstage. The crowd went crazy with cheers and applause.

"And now," he continued, "a hot new act—Sweetbriar, singing songs from their debut CD, *Starring You and Me!*"

Brian and Penny ran onstage and, unbelievably, the clapping got even louder!

Brian launched into the song from *Starring You and Me* that had gotten the most requests—"Blue Eyes."

Funny, but hearing him sing that song didn't hurt anymore. *I guess I really have moved on*, I realized.

Mary-Kate turned to me and gave me a hug.

And then we both started singing along with Brian. Jake wrapped his arm around Mary-Kate. It was nice to see them back together again.

"I'm really glad we helped Brian and Penny after all," I said to Mary-Kate. "Thanks for talking me into it."

Mary-Kate smiled. "I knew you'd be glad," she said. "Hey—I'm just looking out for my sis."

Brian and Penny's next song was a rocker. Mary-Kate and I moved to the beat.

"Favorite things, starting with the letter *D*!" Mary-Kate shouted to Jake and me. "Dancing!"

"Starting with *M*!" Jake added, playing along. "Mary-Kate!"

"Starting with *S*!" I called out. "Sisters!"

We danced the night away to Brian and Penny's music. And hundreds of other people danced with us.

The summer is over,
but the fun is just beginning!
Find out what happens next in

Book 6:
My Best Friend's Boyfriend

"Duck, Ashley!" Brittany said. She crouched down behind a rack full of nightgowns in Mayfield's Department Store and yanked me down beside her.

Brittany and I were trailing Lauren all over the mall, while Mary-Kate was guarding the entrance.

"Spying's hard work!" I said.

Brittany rolled her eyes at me. "Shhh . . . not so loud. She'll hear you."

I peeked out from behind a lacy pink gown. Lauren was holding a pair of black yoga pants in front of her and checking herself out in the mirror. I breathed a sigh of relief. She hadn't spotted us.

"I still feel incredibly guilty about spying on Lauren," I whispered.

"Well, don't," she said. "Not when Lauren tells us that she can't hang out because of a dentist appointment, and then turns up at the mall." She peered out. "Oh, no! What's she doing?"

"Buying some new clothes?" I guessed. "That's what people do in department stores."

Brittany gasped. "No, she's leaving. Come on!"

Trying to keep a low profile, we got up and followed Lauren out of the store. It was so crowded that it was hard to keep track of her. Suddenly, we realized we were following a complete stranger.

"Oh, no, we lost her!" Brittany said. "Quick, Ashley—call Mary-Kate and tell her to be on the lookout."

I took out my cell phone and speed-dialed my sister. "Mary-Kate! We lost Lauren. Do you see her anywhere?"

Mary-Kate giggled. "No sign of her. But I'll keep my eyes peeled."

"Okay. We're coming over. We'll meet you by the fountain."

Brittany and I raced to the fountain near the main entrance. When we got there, we collapsed onto a bench. A few minutes later, we saw Mary-Kate weaving her way through the crowd. She was wearing her darkest pair of sunglasses and her shiniest red lip gloss—total undercover chic.

"Any luck?" Mary-Kate asked.

Brittany shook her head. "Nope, looks like she's—no, wait, there she is!" she exclaimed, pointing toward the food court.

The three of us tiptoed over to the entrance of the food court for a closer look and hid behind some potted palm trees.

"She's waving to someone," Mary-Kate said breathlessly. "Look, it's a guy! I can't see his face, but he looks really familiar…."

We watched as Lauren went over to the mystery guy's table and sat down. She looked really happy.

"Oh, wow!" Brittany squealed. "They're kissing!"

As I watched the scene unfold, I felt the air rush out of me. That was no ordinary guy Lauren was kissing.

It was Ben.

My ex-boyfriend.

The summer is over, but the fun is just beginning!

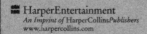

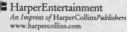

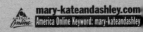

eading Checklist

ndashley

ngle book!

Available wherever books are sold, or call 1-800-331-3761 to order.

Mary-Kate and Ashley

Hit TV Series... is a *New York Times* Bestselling Book Series!

mary-kate olsen   ashley olsen

so little time

secret crush

Win a
**Secret Crush
Prize Pack!**
Details Inside.

It's
What
YOU
Read.

BASED
ON THE HIT
TV SERIES

mary-kateandashley.com
America Online Keyword: mary-kateandashley

Chloe and Riley. . . So much to do. . . **so little tim**

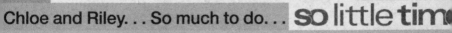

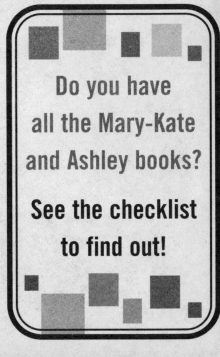

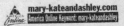